CLAUDIA MAKES UP HER MIND

**Other books by
Ann M. Martin**

Leo the Magnificat
Rachel Parker, Kindergarten Show-off
Eleven Kids, One Summer
Ma and Pa Dracula
Yours Turly, Shirley
Ten Kids, No Pets
Slam Book
Just a Summer Romance
Missing Since Monday
With You and Without You
Me and Katie (the Pest)
Stage Fright
Inside Out
Bummer Summer

THE KIDS IN MS. COLMAN'S CLASS series
BABY-SITTERS LITTLE SISTER series
THE BABY-SITTERS CLUB mysteries
THE BABY-SITTERS CLUB series
CALIFORNIA DIARIES series

CLAUDIA MAKES UP
HER MIND

Ann M. Martin

AN
APPLE
PAPERBACK

SCHOLASTIC INC.
New York Toronto London Auckland Sydney

Cover art by Hodges Soileau

No part of this publication may be reproduced in whole or in part, or stored in a retrieval system, or transmitted in any form or by any means, electronic, mechanical, photocopying, recording, or otherwise, without written permission of the publisher. For information regarding permission, write to Scholastic Inc., Attention: Permissions Department, 555 Broadway, New York, NY 10012.

ISBN 0-590-05991-2

12 11 10 9 8 7 6 5 4 3 2 1   7 8 9/9 0 1 2/0

Printed in the U.S.A.   40

First Scholastic printing, November 1997

*The author gratefully acknowledges
Peter Lerangis
for his help in
preparing this manuscript.*

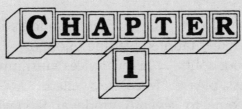

CHAPTER 1

" 'So remember your litterquette: If you drop it, pick it up,' " read my homeroom teacher, Ms. Pilley, from a sheet of paper. " 'Together we can make Stoneybrook Middle School a trash-free zone in November.' "

Litterquette? As in, litter-etiquette?

Puh-leeze.

I hate homeroom announcements. Especially dumb ones. Frankly, that early in the morning, I would much rather be at home, listening to the sound track of my dreams.

"Now, let's see, I have another message here somewhere," Ms. Pilley said, searching the mess on her desk.

My eyes were closing. My mind was going, going . . .

"Eeeewwww! Brandon's throwing spitballs!"

Zing. Wide awake.

Thank you, Bonnie Lasher, class alarm clock.

"Am not!" Brandon Klein retorted.

1

"Then what's this disgusting thing in my hair with *your* bad breath on it?" Bonnie shot back.

"You smelled a spitball?" asked Michael King.

"How do *you* know what Brandon's breath smells like?" taunted Nadine Luongo.

"Oooooooohh . . ." a few voices murmured.

"Class, please!" Ms. Pilley yelled.

Welcome to seventh grade at Stoneybrook Middle School in Stoneybrook, Connecticut. Where spitball throwing is an art and every head is a target.

Well, Brandon was not going to slime my hair. Not after I'd spent all morning braiding it.

I gave him a hard Look. He blushed, shrugged sheepishly, and turned away.

I, Claudia Kishi, have that power over my classmates.

Don't get the wrong impression. I am not a two-hundred-pound weight lifter and I do not have fangs. What I do have is, well, *age*.

You see, I'm thirteen, which is approximately a year older than everyone in my class. Yes, I'm supposed to be in eighth grade. In fact, I *was* in eighth grade at the beginning of the year, but my teachers sent me back. Why? So they wouldn't have to give me a "Clueless" on my report card.

Okay, I'm exaggerating. According to my

guidance counselor, Mrs. Amer, I'm "right-brain overdeveloped," which is a polite way of saying I'm really good in art but I can't spell or do math.

My genius sister, Janine, just calls me "brain-dead." She's in high school but she takes college courses in subjects I've never heard of. My parents are smart too. Mom's a librarian and Dad's an investment banker. So what happened to me? Well, I have a theory. You see, my grandmother, Mimi, was sensitive and artistic. I think her genes skipped a generation and reached me. (Janine insists that can't happen, but obviously this is the one time in her life when she is wrong.) Mimi was very Old World. She was born and raised in Japan. You might not think she and I would have much in common, but we were soul mates. I felt so lost when she died.

Boy, did I want to cry on Mimi's shoulder when I was sent back to seventh grade. I thought I'd ruined the Kishi name forever. I felt humiliated and stupid. And I was devastated about leaving my best friends.

But I've changed. Now I'm glad it happened. First of all, my left brain is doing just fine. My grades are good and I'm understanding math for the first time in my life. (I really can't spell, though. Some things are just hopeless.) Second of all, I still spend time with my eighth-grade friends, especially the ones who belong to the Baby-sitters Club (more about that later). Third, I've made some incredible new friends — Joanna Fried, Josh Rocker, Jeannie Kim, and Shira Epstein. And last but not least . . . ta-da! I have a steady boyfriend. His name is Mark Jaffe, and he sits next to me in homeroom.

That morning, however, he wasn't exactly sitting. *Slumping*, maybe. His head was on his desk, and he was using his forearms as a pillow.

My first instinct was to nudge him awake. But I listened to my second instinct instead, which was to sit still. Ms. Pilley was approaching him with an icy stare, which meant he was dead meat no matter what I did.

"AHEM!" she said.

Mark opened his eyes with a start. "Oh. Sorry."

"You may be the King of the Seventh Grade," said Ms. Pilley, "but in my classroom you are *not* entitled to a royal nap."

The class started tittering. Mark sat up obediently, a pencil at the ready. He looked very earnest and slightly ashamed. But I could tell by his expression that he was soaking up the attention.

What a ham.

A cute ham, though. Mark has the most gorgeous long, brown hair and about a hundred different smiles, each one devastating. Needless to say, he was elected King of the Seventh Grade by a landslide.

The Queen? *Moi.*

How did a seventh-grade newcomer like me become so popular so quickly? With a lot of help from my friends, especially Josh. They all campaigned for me. I was kind of embarrassed by the sudden fame, but being Queen was a great way to meet people.

Including a great boyfriend.

"Now, listen up," Ms. Pilley said. "The annual SMS Color War will begin Friday, a week from today, and it will last through the following Friday. Here are the results of last week's balloting . . ."

This I wanted to hear. I love the SMS Color War. It's a competition among the sixth, seventh, and eighth grades — sports contests, spelling bees, bake sales, weird games, anything goes. The winning class receives a check from the Stoneybrook Chamber of Commerce, to be donated to charity. Each class chooses two things: a color, which all members have to wear during the competitions, and a charity to donate the proceeds to.

Ms. Pilley listed the three chosen charities (ours was the Stoneybrook Adult Literacy Program), and then continued, " 'The eighth grade chose the color blue; the sixth grade, white; and the seventh grade, orange.' "

Clank went my jaw as it hit the desktop.

Orange?

The entire class was going to have to wear *orange?*

Who on earth looks good in orange?

Maybe a circus clown.

"You must be joking," I murmured.

Ms. Pilley looked up. "Is something wrong?"

"No," I lied.

RRRRRRIIING! went the homeroom bell.

" 'Volunteers are still needed for all positions, including events coordinators for each grade'!" Ms. Pilley shouted frantically as we sprang up from our seats.

I gathered my books and headed out the door toward my locker.

I was in a daze. All I could see was a vision of myself in a carrot-colored jumpsuit.

As you might have guessed, I'm very particular about what I wear. In my opinion, every outfit tells a story. That day, for instance, I was wearing a dark plaid skirt I'd picked up in a thrift shop; purple leggings; high, lace-up boots; a long-sleeved, white linen shirt with a solid black tie; and an oversized man's vest. (My hair, in case you were wondering, was in one long braid down my back, with a solitary cornrow hanging off my temple on the left side.) One look and you'd know a lot of my qualities: fun loving, creative, many layered.

6

I was not happy about having to impersonate a citrus fruit for a week.

Mark was walking beside me, chatting with a couple of other friends, but I wasn't really paying attention.

We rounded the corner to our lockers. Josh, Joanna, Jeannie, and Shira were there, gabbing away. They fell silent when they saw my gloomy expression.

"Don't tell me," Josh said. "Let me guess. You flunked homeroom."

Joanna nudged him in the ribs. "Rocker, can't you ever be serious?"

"Uh-oh," Josh murmured, looking from Mark to me. "You two aren't breaking up, are you?"

"Jo-o-osh!" Shira looked mortified.

"Claudia?" Mark asked.

"Orange," I blurted out, violently spinning the dial of my lock. "For a whole week, we all have to look like . . . like . . . "

"Pumpkins?" Josh suggested.

"Exactly," I said.

"Very seventies," Jeannie remarked with a grimace.

"I like orange," Joanna volunteered.

"No way!" exclaimed Josh. "We should have chosen . . . uh, what did you vote for, Claudia?"

"Black," I said.

"Black," Josh declared.

Shira and Joanna rolled their eyes. I could tell Josh was trying to cheer me up, but it wasn't working.

Mark put his arm around me. "I think you look great in any color, Claudia."

"True," said Jeannie with a smile.

"Awwwww," said Shira and Joanna.

Josh groaned. "So! How about those Mets?" (That's Josh-ese for "I'm bored" or "Can we change the topic of conversation?")

"Mets?" Mark asked.

"Just ignore Josh," Shira suggested. "He overdosed on Cocoa Puffs this morning and it affected his brain."

"If you're upset about the color, Claudia," Josh said, "then change it."

"How?" I asked.

Josh shrugged. "Hey, you're the Queen of the Seventh Grade, right? What you say goes."

"The Queen's in charge of the prom, not the Color War," I informed him, taking the books out of my locker.

"You could be in charge of it if you wanted to," Joanna spoke up. "The announcement said the Color War needed events coordinators."

"Still? With only a week to go?" Jeannie asked. "I can't believe no one volunteered."

"Too much work," Shira said.

Josh sighed dramatically. "School spirit ain't what it used to be."

"Joanna, you're a joiner," Mark said. "*You* volunteer."

Joanna shook her head. "I'm already doing too much stuff — class president, yearbook, band . . ."

Click, went my locker as I shut it.

Click, went the lightbulb in my brain.

Joanna's idea made sense. Why shouldn't I be in charge? I mean, the Queen should do *something* for her class. Besides, I wasn't too involved in after-school activities. In fact, I had none. I'd planned it that way, so I could have plenty of time to study. But now that my grades were okay, I could probably handle this.

And so could Mark, for that matter. He had no activities either.

This would be a perfect Royal Project.

"We'll both do it," I said, taking Mark's hand.

Mark looked horrified. *"Whaaaat?"*

"The King and Queen leading the Color War!" Jeannie exclaimed. "What a cute idea."

"But I — I can't," Mark stammered. "I'm . . . busy."

Josh nodded understandingly. "All that extracurricular hanging out."

"She's not asking you to go *to* war, Mark," Shira said.

"But — but —" Mark said.

"Come on, it'll be fun," I urged him.

"I'll do it with you if Mark won't," Josh piped up.

Mark silently dumped some books in his pack and closed his locker door. He took a deep breath and returned all our expectant looks. "Well, I'll think about it, I guess."

"All riiiiight," Joanna exclaimed.

Mark raised an eyebrow and began walking toward class. " 'All right . . . *Sire,*' " he corrected Joanna.

I bumped him with my hip. Josh and Shira groaned. Jeannie and Joanna exchanged a Look.

I wanted to run to the office to volunteer right away, but the first-period bell clanged. We scattered to our classes.

I vowed to go to the office as soon as I could.

I'd never been in charge of a war before.

How cool.

CHAPTER 2

"Candy corn!" I exclaimed, pulling a huge bag of it out of my desk drawer.

"Feed me feed me feed me!" droned Abby Stevenson, who was sitting on my bedroom floor.

I tossed the bag to her and started pulling more stuff from my backpack. "Marshmallow jack-o'-lanterns . . . orange lollipops . . . Doritos . . . orange soda . . . carrots . . ."

"Carrots?"

Six bewildered pairs of eyes stared at me. They belonged to my first group of best friends — the members of the Baby-sitters Club.

Our Friday meeting was about to start, and I was doing my usual duty as vice-president: feeding everyone junk food. Junk food happens to be one of my great passions, right up there with art, cool clothes, and Nancy Drew mysteries. The worse the food is for your health, the more I love it. If my parents knew about all the cookies, pretzels, chips, and candy I hide in my room, they would pass out.

Which is why the carrots took everyone by surprise.

"Anyone recognize a pattern?" I said.

Duh, said the faces of Abby, Kristy Thomas, Stacey McGill, Mary Anne Spier, Jessica Ramsey, and Mallory Pike.

"They're orange!" I blurted out. "The color of the seventh grade, which is going to whup everyone else in the Color War! And guess who is going to be the class events coordinator?"

"Wait," Kristy said. "Is this new business?"

Leave it to Kristy. She's the club president, and she's a stickler for rules. "Well, yeah," I said, "technically, but —"

"Then save it for the meeting," Kristy interrupted.

"Kristyyyy," Stacey said. "We can start. It's time."

"It's five twenty-nine," Kristy corrected her.

The moment she said that, my clock clicked to 5:30.

"*Now,* this meeting will come to order!" shouted Kristy.

"Picky, picky," grumbled Stacey.

"Anyway —" I began.

"Any . . . new . . . business?" said Kristy pointedly.

Abby threw a lollipop wrapper at her. "This is a club, not a dictatocracy."

"Dictatocracy?" Mary Anne repeated.

"*Ship*," said Mallory. "Dictator*ship*."

We were off and running. Chaos as usual. Sometimes I think the BSC is more of a loony bin than a club *or* a dictatorship.

We meet three times a week, Mondays, Wednesdays, and Fridays, from five-thirty until six. Local parents phone us during those times to book baby-sitting jobs. Our clients love us. With one call, they reach seven reliable, experienced sitters (nine, if you count our associate members). And we sitters have a great excuse to get together and gab.

I'm the only BSC member with a private phone line, so my bedroom is the official club headquarters, which is the main reason I'm club vice-president. What are my duties, besides being host and caterer? Nothing, really. Well, I guess I take over if Kristy is ever overthrown, but I'm not too worried about that.

Just kidding.

Kristy isn't really a dictator. She's actually a friendly and fun-loving person. No one minds her bossiness (much). Her brain functions on a different plane than everyone else's. It spills over with ideas, twenty-four hours a day. No problem is too tough for her to solve.

Kristy's greatest solution to a problem? The Baby-sitters Club! Once upon a time, Mrs. Thomas was having trouble finding a sitter for Kristy's younger brother, David Michael. Neither Kristy nor her two older brothers, Charlie and Sam, could sit that night. (Kristy's dad was long gone. He abandoned the family when David Michael was a baby.) Anyway, after watching her mom make one unsuccessful phone call after the other — *bing!* — Kristy had her brilliant idea. The BSC was born.

Kristy, Mary Anne, Stacey, and I were the original members, but the calls poured in and we had to expand fast. Kristy made sure we wouldn't be overwhelmed. She set us up like a company, with officers, dues, and a scheduling system. We share jobs equally, and we keep each other up-to-date about our clients by writing up each sitting job in an official BSC notebook.

Kristy is fantastic with kids. She's constantly dreaming up cool kid-related ideas — holiday events, contests, theme parties. She even formed a softball team of BSC charges, called Kristy's Krushers. (They compete against Bart's Bashers, a team led by a guy who used to be Kristy's sort-of boyfriend, Bart Taylor.)

You can recognize Kristy instantly at a BSC meeting. She's the short, fashion-challenged brunette with the big mouth. Okay, to be fair,

14

her clothes look fine, but I believe I will die of shock if I ever see her wear anything besides jeans and turtlenecks. When Kristy's mom got married again, to this rich guy named Watson Brewer, I thought Kristy might start to shop high-end, but no-o-o-o.

Kristy used to live across the street from me but nowadays she lives in Watson's mansion, *way* across town (her brother Charlie has to drive her to BSC meetings). You would not believe the size of the house. You would also not believe how crowded it is. Kristy has a two-and-a-half-year-old sister, Emily Michelle, who was adopted from Vietnam. Kristy's grandmother, Nannie, moved in after Emily Michelle's arrival to help with child care. And Watson's two kids from a previous marriage, Andrew and Karen, live in the house during alternate months. Add one pet from just about every phylum known to science, and you have an idea of life with the Brewer/Thomases.

I missed Kristy a lot when she moved. But the person who was really devastated was Mary Anne Spier. She and Kristy have been best friends since birth. They grew up next door to each other. People sometimes say they look like sisters, which is sort of true. Mary Anne's hair is shorter, though, and she dresses in preppier clothes. As far as personality goes, they might as well come from different planets.

Mary Anne is as quiet, sweet, and sensitive as Kristy is loud and domineering. If you have a personal problem, Kristy will try to solve it instantly, but Mary Anne will make you feel better, just by listening and sympathizing.

If the BSC were a body, Kristy would be the mind and Mary Anne would be the legs. As secretary, Mary Anne makes the club run. She keeps the BSC record book, which contains a job calendar and an up-to-date list of client information: names, addresses, phone numbers, rates paid, and children's ages. When a call comes in, Mary Anne knows at a glance who's available for the job. That's because she also marks down every one of our conflicts on the calendar, including lessons, after-school activities, doctor appointments, family trips, and so on.

If I had to do Mary Anne's job, I'd probably have a heart attack. We are so different. Well, except for one thing: We're the only BSC members who have steady boyfriends. Mary Anne's is a guy named Logan Bruno. He's an associate member of the BSC, which means he helps out when we're super busy, but he doesn't have to attend meetings or pay dues. Which is too bad because we like having him around. He's a good guy, and he also embarrasses easily in a roomful of girls.

Mary Anne definitely picked up her organizational skills from her dad, Richard. For years, he ran Mary Anne's life on a strict schedule. I mean, up to the minute. He made my parents look lenient. According to Mary Anne, he was always worried about being a perfect single parent. You see, Mary Anne's mom died when Mary Anne was a baby, and Mary Anne's grandparents wanted custody of her. They thought Richard couldn't handle being a single father.

People have been underestimating poor Richard his whole life. Back in high school he had a girlfriend named Sharon whose parents thought he wasn't good enough. How do I know this? Because he's married to her now.

That story is right out of a soap opera. Remember when I said the BSC had to expand? Well, one of our new members was a girl named Dawn Schafer, who'd just moved here from California with her brother and their newly divorced mom. Mrs. Schafer was a Stoneybrook native named — you guessed it — Sharon. When Dawn and Mary Anne discovered the ancient connection, they reintroduced the former lovebirds. The electricity was still there, I guess. They married, and Mary Anne and her dad moved into the Schafers' farmhouse.

The marriage has been great for Richard. He's loosened up a lot. It was great for Mary

Anne too, until Dawn moved back to California to live with her dad (following her brother, who had done the same thing earlier). Now Mary Anne feels siblingless again. Sob, sob. (I told you it was a soap opera.)

Dawn is now our honorary member. We all love and miss her, even though her move was rough on our schedule. We were swamped with the extra work. We didn't even have time to look for a new member.

But one fell into our laps.

That was Abby Stevenson. She moved from Long Island into a house on Kristy's street, with her twin sister, Anna, and their mom. (Mrs. Stevenson works for a New York City publishing company. Mr. Stevenson, sadly, died in a car accident when the girls were nine.) Kristy invited both Abby and Anna to a BSC meeting, and we asked them to join the club. Abby agreed but Anna said no (she wants to be a professional violinist and spends most of her spare time practicing).

Sometimes it's hard to believe Abby and Anna are identical twins. Abby is outgoing and hilarious. She's a fantastic natural athlete, her hair cascades in ringlets to her shoulders, she's allergic to just about everything, and she has asthma. Anna is quiet and thoughtful. Her favorite sport is dragging a bow across a fiddle and her hair is short. She's not allergic or asthmatic, but she does have a severe spine curvature problem that Abby doesn't have, called scoliosis.

Abby and Anna became our good friends right away. They invited all of us to their Bat Mitzvah. That's an important ceremony many Jewish girls go through at age thirteen, to symbolize their passage into womanhood. Abby and Anna had to recite in Hebrew, which was pretty mind-boggling.

Abby is our alternate officer, which means she takes over the duties of any officer who's absent from a meeting.

As I passed around my orange treats, Abby was munching thoughtfully on a marshmallow pumpkin. "Just think," she said, "if you were still in eighth grade, you'd have to find blue food."

"Blueberries," Jessi suggested.

"Bluefish," Kristy chipped in.

"Gross," said Mallory.

Stacey swallowed a mouthful of Doritos. "No offense, Claudia, but *orange*? I mean, were you in your right minds? What's your charity, Fashion Victims of America?"

"Tell me about it," I said with a sigh.

I knew Stacey would feel the same way I did. She is my best friend in the world. We both love clothes. We also love to shop together, even though she buys from boutiques and I raid the thrift shops. She likes sleek, urban high fashion. Black is her absolute favorite color. It sets off her golden blonde hair and fair complexion.

Stacey likes to say she picked up her fashion sense in New York City. She grew up there, until her father's company relocated him to Connecticut. That was when Stacey joined the BSC. Since then she's moved back to NYC and back to Stoneybrook again. Along the way, unfortunately, her parents divorced. Her dad stayed in the Big Apple, so she often takes the train there for visits.

After the divorce, Stacey tried so hard to please both parents that she became sick. She aggravated this condition she has, called diabetes. Stacey has explained it to me a million times, and I think I finally have it straight: Basically, when you eat sugar, your body's supposed to store some of it, then release a little at a time into your bloodstream. But in a diabetic, the sugar zooms right into the blood, like jumping into a freezing ocean instead of inching in to get used to it. If Stacey eats one candy bar, her body could go into shock. How does she deal with this? Fine. She has to eat meals at regular times, stay away from refined sugar (the carrots in my backpack were for Stacey), and inject herself daily with a hormone called insulin. (I know, it sounds like torture, especially that last part. But Stacey deals with it well and leads an active, normal life filled with lots of energetic shopping.)

I don't know how Stacey can stand to be around a chocoholic like me. Oh, well, I guess even best friends can have major differences. Actually, we have two. The other one is math aptitude. Stacey is a whiz. (She actually scored the highest in the whole state in a math team competition.)

Because of those math skills, Stacey is the club treasurer. She collects dues each Monday and stores the money in a manila envelope. Once a month she pays our expenses — including part of my phone bill, gas money for Charlie, and supplies for Kid-Kits. And occasionally she'll allow us to spend leftover money on a pizza party.

Now you know our senior officers. Stacey, Kristy, Mary Anne, and Abby are all thirteen, like me. (Unlike me, they are in eighth grade.)

Jessi and Mallory are our junior officers. They're best friends. They both adore horse books, and each of them has a cool creative talent. Jessi's is dance. She takes tons of lessons, practices all the time, and has performed in ballets. Mallory loves to write and illustrate her own stories.

Why do we call Jessi and Mallory junior officers? Because they're eleven and in sixth grade and their parents won't let them baby-sit at night, unless it's for their own siblings. (Boy, do they grumble about that.)

Actually, Jessi and Mal are more mature than most seventh-graders I know. Maybe that's because they're each the oldest kid in the family. Jessi has a sister and a baby brother, and Mallory has seven siblings. (Yup, seven, including very loud boy triplets. Mature? I'm surprised she doesn't have gray hair!)

Physically Jessi and Mal are not alike at all. Mallory's skin is creamy white and freckled, and her hair is a mass of reddish-brown curls. Jessi has chocolate-brown skin and she keeps her black hair pulled back in a tight bun.

Jessi, by the way, grew up in a racially mixed neighborhood in Oakley, New Jersey. Unfortunately, when her family moved here, they found that Stoneybrook was not exactly multi-cultural. Some of their neighbors gave them a hard time, just because the Ramseys are black. (We Kishis have faced this kind of stupidity too.) Things have managed to work out, though. Sometimes even prejudiced people can change.

Anyway, that's it for our regular members. We also have two associate members. As I mentioned before, Logan Bruno is one of them. The other is Shannon Kilbourne. She goes to a local private school called Stoneybrook Day School.

Too bad she doesn't go to SMS. She's a real joiner. She'd have great ideas for the Color War.

At this point, I could have used a consultant.

"I don't know how I'm going to pull this together fast enough," I said, looking at a roomful of chomping orange mouths. "Mark didn't want to help me out at first, but I think I convinced him."

"Maybe you guys can set up a kissing contest," Abby suggested. "You can compete to break the Guinness record. Longest liplock."

I could feel myself blush. Jessi and Mallory were dissolving into giggles.

Kristy did not look amused. She's a little sensitive about the topic of Mark. She and Mark's friend Steve double dated with Mark and me not long ago, and it was a disaster.

I was relieved when Mary Anne changed the subject. "When I sat for the Barrett/DeWitt kids the other day, I mentioned the Color War. You should have seen the look on Suzi Barrett's face."

"She hates orange too?" Stacey asked.

"No, she wanted to have a *family* Color War," Mary Anne replied. "They all did. But they couldn't agree on colors before I had to leave."

Kristy was sitting forward on the edge of her

chair. Her eyes were wide, her lips curled up into a half smile.

I knew that look. Kristy's brain was cooking up something.

"That's a great idea!" she said.

"What?" Abby asked.

"I move we plan for a Kids' Color War. Just for our charges."

Abby looked impressed. "Hey, I second that motion."

"All in favor?" Kristy asked.

"AYE!" we called out in unison.

Kristy grabbed a pencil and a sheet of paper. "Okay, let's think of a few events before the phone rings. . . ."

CHAPTER 3

SHOW YOUR COLORS
AT THE 35TH ANNUAL
STONEYBROOK MIDDLE SCHOOL
COLOR WAR!

IDEAS NEEDED IMMEDIATELY FOR EVENTS.
CONTACT THE FOLLOWING EVENTS COORDINATORS:
GRADE 8: Alan Gray
GRADE 7: Claudia Kishi & mark gaffee
GRADE 6: Sara Erickson

"*A*lan Gray?" I murmured. "That name wasn't there yesterday."

It was Tuesday morning. I'd arrived at school early to collect ideas for Color War events from students. I was hanging out by the poster, pen in hand, with Josh, Shira, Jeannie, and Joanna.

How many kids had volunteered ideas so far? Two. One suggested a pinball tournament, the other an arm-wrestling match.

With this kind of imagination, we were in big trouble.

But now I was more concerned about something else. I was going to have to lead my class against the biggest dork of the eighth grade.

"Who's Alan Gray?" Josh asked. "An old boyfriend or something?"

I almost barfed. "Alan Gray is the absolute lowest form of life on the planet," I explained. "Amoebas run away when they see him."

"Amoebas don't have legs," Josh said.

"You know what I mean," I snapped.

"Claudia?" Joanna said. "Mark's name doesn't look right somehow."

"It's Mark with a *k*, not a *c*," I explained. "I made that mistake once before."

"Uh, hello? Homeroom is starting soon?" Shira said. "If no one's going to give us ideas, fine. Write ours down, at least, Claudia. Num-

ber one. How about a bake-off? Everyone sub-
mits baked goods."

"I'll do chocolate chip cookies," Jeannie said.

"Mississippi mud fudge cake," Josh piped
up.

"You can make that?" Shira asked.

Josh looked crushed. "I have to make it?"

"How about a writing contest?" suggested
Jeannie. "The seventh grade could win that, no
sweat. Like, limericks or something."

"Great," I replied.

— *Limrix*

I wrote.

"Weird foot races!" Joanna said. "You know,
three-legged, blindfolded . . ."

"I *love* those!" I said.

"An art contest!" Josh blurted out.

"Now you're talking!" I let out a whoop and
flung my arms around him.

When I let go, Josh's face was red.

Shira looked about ready to crack up. "Uh,
Joshie? Are you feeling all right?"

"You look a little flushed," Jeannie remarked.

"No, I'm —" Josh's voice broke off in a
squeak. He swallowed and tried again. "I'm
fine."

"How about those Mets, Josh?" Jeannie
asked.

Boy, do they love to tease him.

"I have one!" Shira blurted out. "A hog-calling contest!"

"Hog-calling?" Jeannie and I said at the same time.

"My cousins in Nebraska do it," Shira insisted. "Like this: *SOOOOO-EEEEEEE!*"

I thought I would never recover my hearing.

Bravely I kept writing. As ideas flew at me from all sides, I scribbled down as many as I could:

— chest match
— stilt race
— battel of the rock bands
— best originle outfit
— race to pull 100 yards of dentle flos across football feild

(That was Josh's idea, of course.)

— janiter's mop toss
— hi score on vidio game to be agrede on

"It's one *e*," Mark's voice said.

I looked up. Mark was there, smiling at me.

"Oh, hi!" I exclaimed. "Thanks."

I crossed out the last *e* of *agrede*.

"No, I mean my last name," Mark said, gesturing toward the sign. "It's J-A-F-F-E."

Ugh. Just when I thought it was safe to stop feeling like a dunce.

"Sorry," I murmured.

"No problem," Mark said, wrapping an arm around my shoulder. "You can make it up to me."

"Didn't I hear that line in a bad movie?" Josh asked.

Shira gave him a shove. "Josh was just going to the bathroom. Right, Josh?"

"Well," Jeannie said, backing away, "I guess we'll leave you two alone."

She pulled at Joanna and Shira, and they all scurried down the hall, giggling.

Mark and I began strolling toward homeroom.

It was kind of funny. I mean, why were they acting so embarrassed? What did they expect us to do? Start making out in the hallway, two minutes before homeroom?

"What movie was he talking about?" Mark asked.

"Josh?" I said. "Oh, just ignore him."

"No, really. He's always saying stuff like that."

"He just has a weird sense of humor."

Mark shrugged. "Whatever."

"So, what are your ideas for the Color War?"

"Ideas?" Mark laughed. "That's your department."

"Anyone can think of ideas, Mark."

"I don't know. Football, I guess."

"A game? Or, like, individual competition — throwing a ball the farthest, or coolest helmet . . ."

"Yeah. Whatever."

I took a deep breath. I had figured I'd be working harder on the Color War than Mark would. I don't mind that. Mark's not exactly a joiner. But he's not a slacker either. I was hoping he'd at least have a few ideas.

"Mark, are you sure you want to do this?" I asked.

"Yes, Claudia," Mark replied. "I told you I would. I mean, do we need to have it all planned *now*?"

"No, but —"

"I'll think about it. I'll help out."

"Help out? But we're supposed to be —"

The homeroom bell cut me off before I could say *co-coordinators*.

We were turning into Ms. Pilley's room now. One of Mark's buddies was rushing in behind us. He slapped Mark on the shoulder and they both started talking about some pro sports game.

Was I too stressed about the Color War? Maybe Mark was right. Maybe I should relax.

As I walked to my desk, I noticed a folded sheet of paper.

Brandon Klein Alert. Last time this happened, I opened the sheet to find a note in his handwriting that read, "At 8:07, everyone blow your nose."

I sat down and quickly hid the note in my lap. When I was sure Ms. Pilley was looking away, I unfolded it and read:

Stoneybrook Middle School
Guidance Department
Memo from Mrs. Florence Amer
To Claudia Kishi

Claudia,
   Would you please come see me immediately after school today, Tuesday, on a matter of some urgency?
                         Yours,
                         Mrs. Amer

Oh. My. Lord.
I couldn't breathe.
I almost dropped the sheet.
Most students only see Mrs. Amer once a year, in June. She smiles, pats you on the back, and says good luck in your new grade. If you're called in before the end of the year, you worry.

This year, I'd been called in once before. The

31

day Mrs. Amer sent me back to seventh grade.

What now?

Take it easy, Kishi, I told myself. *Calm down. Maybe it's no big deal.*

Right.

And the world is flat.

CHAPTER 4

"It's probably nothing," Jeannie said.

I gripped her arm tightly as we turned the corner toward the guidance office. My other arm was clutching Stacey's. Mary Anne and Shira flanked us on either side. Behind us were Josh, Kristy, Joanna, Abby, Jessi, and Mallory.

A procession. That's what it felt like. A procession to a public hanging.

I had told my seventh-grade friends about the note during lunch. I'd told my eighth-grade friends right after, as they walked into the cafeteria for eighth-grade lunch. They must have passed the word to Jessi and Mal.

I hadn't wanted to make a big deal about it. I'd tried to mention the note casually. No big emotional traumas.

I guess they could tell how I really felt. Because they'd showed up at my locker after school.

Now, with all of them surrounding me, I could not hold it back. I was petrified.

"I can't do this," I muttered.

"Maybe it's just a progress report," Mary Anne suggested.

"I mean, my grades aren't *that* bad," I said. "Are they?"

"Maybe she's just checking up on you," Kristy suggested. "Finding out how you like seventh grade."

"Tell her the teachers stink but the kids are great," Josh said.

"Okay, my last English test wasn't so wonderful," I continued, "but I passed. And I'm doing okay in math and history."

"Better than okay," Stacey agreed.

"Better than me," Shira added.

"That's not saying much," Josh remarked.

"This is no time to joke," Jeannie called over her shoulder.

"Hey, I'm just trying to cheer Claudia up," Josh protested.

I stopped walking about halfway down the corridor. A few yards away, the door to the guidance office was open. Voices were filtering out. One of them was Mrs. Amer's.

My heart was pounding. I was having a flashback. A flashback to the day Mrs. Amer dropped the bomb.

"What if she's going to do it again?" My voice was all parched and whispery.

"Do what again?" Abby asked.

"Send me back," I said.

Jeannie looked bewildered. "To *sixth grade*?"

"It's not so bad, you know," Jessi spoke up.

"At this rate, someone ought to notify the kindergarten teachers," I went on. "They're going to have to squeeze a big chair into the art corner."

"Claudia-a-a-a," Mallory said.

"If this were something really serious," Stacey added, "your parents would have been called in."

"Maybe they *are* in there," I replied.

Josh took me gently by the shoulder. "Don't worry, Claudia. Whatever happens, we'll all stand by you. If you want, I'll tell Mrs. Amer how much you help us in class, how hard you work —"

"Yo, what's going on?" a familiar deep voice called out from behind me.

Mark. Just the person I wanted to see.

I spun away from Josh and pushed through my crowd of friends. "Oh, Mark. I'm a wreck. A total wreck. I'm so glad you're here."

I threw my arms around him.

He seemed a little stunned. "Whoa, what happened?"

"You know . . . the note," I replied, my face buried in his flannel shirt.

"Oh, right," Mark said. "From the guidance lady. Uh-oh."

"Yo, Jaffe!" yelled another voice from down the hall.

"Oooh, no PDAs in the hallway!" said someone else.

"Markie and Claudia, sitting in a tree . . ."

"Just shut up, will you?" Shira shouted. "Babies."

I looked toward the voices. Two of Mark's friends, Frank O'Malley and Tom Blanton, were at the end of the hallway, grinning at us.

"Be right there," Mark called over his shoulder. Then he gave me a quick squeeze. "Look, Claudia. It's okay. Really. I mean, she's probably, like, giving you a new locker or something."

"Guidance counselors don't do that," I said.

Mark shrugged. "Or whatever. You know. Listen, I have to go to Frank's, okay? He's moving to Oregon soon, so —"

"I know," I said. "It's okay."

"But call me. I really want to know. And don't worry, all right?"

"All right."

Mark smiled and ran his fingers gently through my hair. Then he turned and left.

I felt a little better. But I wished he'd stayed.

When I turned around, the first thing I noticed was Josh's face. He was glaring in Mark's direction.

"Sensitive guy," he muttered sarcastically.

"*Jo-o-o-osh*," Shira said.

"He can't help that his best friend in life is moving," I explained as I started walking slowly toward the guidance office door. "Besides, he's probably right. It's nothing to worry about."

"Gee, why didn't we think of that?" Josh murmured.

"Should we wait for you?" Mary Anne asked.

I shook my head. "Nahhh. You guys go ahead home. This might take awhile."

To a chorus of "good lucks" and "don't worrys," I went into the office and found Mrs. Amer's cubicle.

My parents were not there. That was a good sign.

Hope, hope, hope.

Mrs. Amer was sitting at her desk, a telephone cradled on her shoulder. When she saw me, she quickly ended the call. "Hello, Claudia. Please sit."

I did not like the tone of her voice. It seemed lower than normal.

The look on her face wasn't too reassuring either. She seemed preoccupied. Worried. Her brow was all scrunched up, and she wasn't meeting my glance.

Transfer.

Boarding school.

Military academy.

Reform school.

The words flashed through my mind as Mrs. Amer pulled open a file cabinet drawer and took out a folder with my name on it.

I couldn't let her do this to me. This was unfair. I had to say something.

"Mrs. Amer, I've really been trying hard," I blurted out.

"Yes, indeed." Shuffle, shuffle, shuffle went her fingers through my folder.

"I got an A on my last math exam," I said.

"We-e-ell, that must be a nice feeling," Mrs. Amer murmured.

"And an 'Excellent' on my last social studies paper. The one about the Japanese internment camps? I mean, okay, I know my spelling still isn't good. But I work on it. Really. Janine, my sister? She's been making these flash cards. And she says I'm showing improvement. That was one of the words. *Improvement.* I got it right. *I-M-P-R-O* — well, it's easier if it's on paper. . . ."

I was babbling. My mouth was running on its own. I couldn't stop.

Mrs. Amer listened patiently. Finally she

leaned across the desk and said, "Claudia, dear, I *know* how hard you're trying. And I also know you're doing well."

"You do?"

She nodded and began shuffling through my folder again. "Your teachers seem very impressed. Although I do see Ms. Chiavetta's comments about the spelling. Anyway, to tell you the truth, Claudia, I was thinking about moving you again —"

"I'll do better, really!" I blurted out. "What am I going to do about the Color War? To have a Queen of the Seventh Grade who's in sixth grade — I mean, I know it's not supposed to mean much, but I —"

"Pardon me?" Mrs. Amer looked up from the folder to peer at me. "What about sixth grade?"

I gulped. "You said you wanted to move me!"

"I do." Mrs. Amer cocked her head curiously. "Back to *eighth* grade."

Bonnnnng.

I felt as if I'd been hit over the head.

"Eighth?"

"I know it sounds a little ridiculous, yanking you out and then putting you back in," Mrs. Amer went on. "But I've been thinking long and hard about this. I've discussed it with the principal, your teachers, and your parents. We think you have improved rapidly, and are perhaps ready to move on.

I opened my mouth to speak. All that came out was air. Air in shock.

Mrs. Amer began flipping through several reports in the folder. "Your cognitive skills, your creative thinking, your maturity — all are way above your seventh-grade peers. Let me ask you something. Do you feel challenged enough, Claudia?"

"Well . . . um . . . I, uh . . ."

"Here's my thinking," Mrs. Amer said. "You haven't been out of eighth grade for very long. You could probably catch up with a little help. The school will provide you with tutors. *If* you want them. Please understand that I don't want to railroad you. The decision is entirely yours."

She was looking at me expectantly. I swallowed a huge glob of saliva.

The first words that popped into my brain?

GO FOR IT!

I could picture the expression on Stacey's face. She would absolutely faint with joy. I imagined myself making an announcement at a BSC meeting.

I'd be back in eighth grade.

Back where I belong.

That thought lasted about a nanosecond.

Then I thought of Mark. And Jeannie. And

Shira and Joanna and Josh. And my teachers.

And my Queenship.

Was I crazy? I was going to leave my first serious boyfriend? Turn my back on four fantastic friends? Give up the first classes that didn't make me feel like a total doofus? Not to mention tossing aside the throne.

"Do I have to decide now?" I asked.

Mrs. Amer smiled. "Of course not. But I don't want this to drag out too long. The marking period ends soon. Why don't we make an appointment — you, me, and your parents — for sometime next week?"

"Okay, fine," I said. "I'll tell them to call you."

"I know this isn't going to be an easy decision," Mrs. Amer said, standing up. "Please don't hesitate to come see me between now and then. I'm here to help."

I stood up too. "Thanks, Mrs. Amer."

We shook hands and I left.

I was kind of hoping one or two of my friends might have stayed. But the hallway was empty.

I needed to talk to someone — but who? Stacey? Mark? Jeannie?

A seventh-grade friend? An eighth-grade friend? My family?

How could I possibly decide something like this?

CHAPTER 5

Tuesday

Today I baby-sat for Linny and Hannie Papadakis. Their mom was taking Sari to the doctor.

And I sat for Jake, Patsy, and Laurel Kuhn.

I was going to have a nice, simple football toss.

Hide-and-seek.

EASY job.

no sweat.

WHAT Happened?

As you can see, I wasn't the only one who'd had a tough Tuesday.

The afternoon started innocently enough. Abby went right to the Papadakis house after school. Linny Papadakis, who is nine, met Abby at the door. Hannie, his seven-year-old sister, raced into the living room behind him.

"Hiiiiii!" they squealed.

Linny was wearing a black suit, and Hannie had on a black velvet party dress with a black-and-white sash.

"Let me guess . . . a funeral for a doll?" was Abby's greeting.

"No, silly," Hannie said, "this is our color, for the Color War!"

"Cool," Abby replied. "Just getting into the spirit a little early, huh?"

"Come on, let's go," Linny insisted.

"Go where?" Abby asked.

"To Brenner Field. To the *War*."

Abby grinned. Linny loves to think big. If he decides he wants to do something, he goes for it. Even if no one else in the world is going with him.

"Uh, guys," Abby said patiently, "it's not today."

"Yes it is!" Hannie insisted. "Mom said she'd drive us on the way to the doctor."

"I know you're eager," Abby said, "but let's

not hatch our chickens before they're caught. Or whatever. These things don't just *happen*. You have to prepare. Find contestants. Make lists and stuff —"

"Everybody knows," Linny replied. "The Pikes are going . . . Buddy Barrett and his brothers and sisters . . ."

"Whoa, whoa, wait —"

Rrrrriiiing! a phone sounded.

"I'll get it!" called Mrs. Papadakis's voice from upstairs. "Hi, Abby! I'll be right down!"

"We *have* to go," Linny insisted.

"Or we'll tell Mom you should never be our baby-sitter again," Hannie said.

"But — I mean — what do you think you're going to do?" Abby stammered. "What events?"

"*You're* the baby-sitter," Linny replied. "You're supposed to think of them."

"WAAAAAAAHHH!" cried Sari from the top of the stairs. "DON'T WANNA GO TO DOCTOR!"

The wailing became louder as Mrs. Papadakis clomped downstairs, dressed in her office clothes and carrying Sari. "Abby, it's for you. You can take it in the kitchen. . . . What are you two doing in your Sunday clothes? Go change right now!"

"Mo-o-o-om!" Hannie complained.

"Our team color is black!" Linny explained.

44

"WAAAAAAAAAH!" Sari commented.

"Excuse me," said Abby. She raced into the kitchen and picked up the receiver. "Hello?"

On the other end she heard screaming and yelling too.

"Abby, it's Jessi!" Jessi shouted.

"Don't tell me," Abby said. "The Color War, right?"

"They planned all this behind our backs — at school, over the phone —"

"Okay. Okay. We have to calb dowd." Abby's allergies were kicking in. "Dow. A — a — ah-hhh-*choooo!*"

"Are you okay?"

"It's the stress. Or maybe the dust."

"I called Kristy," Jessi said. "She'll meet us at Brenner Field to help out. Mal will come over with her brothers and sisters. Mrs. Arnold, too, and Franklin's home from work —"

"What about evedts? Add prizes add stuff?"

"Buddy and Lindsey thought some up. So did the Pikes. And between Kristy and us — oh, I almost forgot. Kristy told me to ask you: Could you get your mom to donate a box of kids' books to the winning team's charity?"

"By the tibe we get to Bredder Field?"

"No! The kids want this to last a week, like the SMS Color War."

"Okay, I'll ask her todight."

"Great. See you in a few minutes."

Abby hung up and dashed into the living room.

As Mrs. Papadakis bundled Sari up, she gave Abby some last-minute instructions. Soon Hannie raced downstairs, dressed in black sweats. Linny was behind her, wearing a black-and-white plaid sweater and pants decorated with some awful black-costumed superhero.

They all ran outside and piled into the car. Linny and Hannie were practically bouncing out of their seats the whole way.

"I'm going to hit the farthest home run in the history of Stoneybrook!" Linny predicted.

"It's not sports," Hannie said. "It's crafts and stuff."

"No way!"

"Way!"

"Nobody says *way* anymore!"

"WAAAAAAHHH!" screamed Sari.

"Ki-i-i-ids!" said Mrs. Papadakis.

"Sssshh," said Abby.

When they arrived at Brenner Field, the kids raced out of the car. Kristy was already on the baseball diamond, hitting fly balls to Jackie and Shea Rodowsky.

Hannie stopped in her tracks. "It *is* base-ball!"

"Yesss!" Linny cried, running onto the field.

"I udderstad there's a whole list of evetts,"

Abby said, putting her arm around Hannie's shoulder.

"Hi!" came a shout to their left.

Jessi was running onto the field with Jake Kuhn and his sisters, Laurel and Patsy. The kids were all wearing red.

"Can we play soccer?" Jake asked.

Hannie was looking at them curiously. "Hey, you were supposed to be on our team."

"We are," Patsy said.

"But our color is black."

Now the oldest five of the seven Barrett/DeWitt kids were charging toward us.

Two of them wore purple and three wore white.

Abby quickly glanced back toward the ball field. Kristy was rounding up the Rodowsky boys. They were dressed in blue.

"Uh, did anyone consult anyone else about colors?" Abby asked loudly.

Her answer was a sea of shaking heads.

"Uh-oh," Kristy said. "Okay, everybody over here, on the double! Let's form three teams and pick colors."

"What if we're dressed wrong?" Lindsey De-Witt asked.

"I brought a pad of paper and some safety pins in my backpack," Kristy replied. "If you're in the wrong color, wear a sign with the name of the right one."

"Then can we hit home runs?" Linny asked.

"After colors, we discuss events," Kristy said.

"Yea, black all the way!" Linny cried out. He sprinted toward the backstop, where Kristy's backpack was lying in the grass.

"Purple rules!" Buddy screamed, running after him.

"Let's go red!" bellowed Jake.

"Wait? Is that it?" Jackie asked. "But I hate those colors!"

"Too late!" Buddy said.

The Pike kids were now noisily crossing the street toward the field, dressed in shades of orange and yellow.

Abby, Jessi, and Kristy exchanged a weary Look.

The War was raging, and it hadn't even begun.

CHAPTER 6

Beep. "Why aren't you home? Call me!"

Beep. "This is Kristy. Are you still alive?"

Beep. "See, it wasn't as bad as you thought. Or was it?"

My answering machine had fourteen messages when I arrived home Tuesday evening. All of them were from my friends who'd been with me outside Mrs. Amer's office.

Mark hadn't left one, but I wasn't really bothered by that. It's not his style to get all worked up.

Still, I really would have liked to talk to him.

I was a wreck.

My mind felt like a tennis ball, being whacked from one decision to the other.

Whack. Eighth. I wanted to be around my lifelong friends. Kids my own age.

Then, *whack.* I'd flash back to earlier in the year, when I *was* in eighth grade. I'd almost forgotten how I'd felt back then.

Like a total, absolute dunce.

I remember looking at the smart kids in class, the Staceys and Mary Annes, and knowing — *knowing* — that I could never understand schoolwork the way they could.

Don't worry, I used to say to myself. *Artists don't need algebra.* Or social studies. Or whatever class I happened to be in.

Now I knew what lame excuses those were. I was pushing down a deep feeling inside myself. A feeling that I was a big, fat nothing.

Boy, had my life changed since then. In seventh grade, I *was* one of those smart students. Kids were asking *me* for help. I could actually show Mom and Dad my tests without feeling ashamed. Once, when I brought home a perfect math test, Dad called me "an artist and a scholar." Even Janine was jealous.

I liked that feeling. A lot.

I was comfortable in seventh grade. I got good grades. I had friends. I had a boyfriend. I was Queen.

As Kristy says, "If it ain't broke, don't fix it." Easy decision.

So why was I so torn?

Mark. I had to call Mark. He'd help me figure this out.

I remembered he was at Frank O'Malley's. I grabbed the phone book and flipped to the *O* section.

No. I couldn't. Frank's family was moving soon. They were probably busy packing. I didn't want to bother Mark there.

I mean, if he called *me,* that would be another story. . . .

Rrrrriiiing!

I grinned.

Mark had read my mind.

I snatched up the receiver. "Hello?"

"Was I right?"

Stacey's voice. Not Mark's.

I felt let down. *Come on, Kishi, she's your best friend.* "Right about what?" I asked.

"Mrs. Amer! She didn't flunk you, right?"

"No. She wants me to go back to eighth grade."

Stacey fell silent. For a moment I thought we'd been cut off. "Are you kidding?" she finally said.

"Nope."

"Oh my lord. Oh, that is so great! I am so-o-o-o proud of you!"

"Yeah? I guess. It's just that . . . well, I don't know if I want to."

"Wait. You're not serious. Because, Claudia, this is a no-brainer. I mean, you *are* coming back."

"Well, that's what I thought at first too. But now I'm not so sure, Stacey. I like seventh grade. I like my classes. I don't feel so stupid anymore —"

"You won't feel stupid in eighth grade. I mean it. I'll tutor you. We all will."

"But you guys are busy. I don't want to tie you up just because I can't —"

"But that's just it, Claudia. You *can*. You always were smart, you just never knew it. But now you have the confidence. You believe in yourself. That's what seventh grade did for you. And that's all you ever needed. You won't tie us up. We'll tutor you for a week or two, and then you won't need us."

"You think so?"

"Guaranteed. Look, you *have* to be in eighth grade. We have to graduate together. It's not just this year, Claudia. If you stay in seventh grade, you'll be a year behind *our whole lives!*"

Whack.

Suddenly eighth grade didn't seem so bad.

It seemed even better after I talked to Mary Anne, Kristy, Abby, Jessi, and Mal. They all had the same opinion. Yes for eighth grade.

Somewhere in the middle of all that was dinner. That was *another* long discussion. Janine's reaction? "I don't know how you could *want* to stay in middle school another year. Pass the pork chops, please."

Dad said, "I hope you don't base this decision on proximity to a boyfriend." (Huh? I don't even know what proximiting is.)

Mom was nicer. She promised to support whichever decision I made.

But my friends' words were sinking in. They were right. I had to be where I'd started. Where I belonged.

In eighth grade.

As I went back to my room, my heart was somewhere around my toes. My seventh-grade friends were expecting me to call them. Some of them were not going to take this well.

Mark would be hurt. His best friend was leaving town, and now me. How could I do this to him?

I called Jeannie instead.

"Hello?" her voice greeted me.

"Hi, Jeannie? It's Claud."

"Claudia?" she practically shrieked. "I've been so-o-o worried! I thought, you know, since you didn't call, it was some horrible news."

"Well, Mrs. Amer wants to move me back to eighth grade, and I think I'm going to say yes."

"Wha-a-a-at? You're not serious?"

"I am."

"Oh . . . that *is* horrible news," Jeannie murmured. "I mean, it's good news, for you. I guess. I mean, you can skip over the rest of seventh grade?"

"But I've already been through seventh grade."

"You once told me you didn't remember anything you learned in seventh grade the first time around. So that's a *whole year* you have to catch up on."

Ugh. I hadn't looked at it that way. Most of seventh grade — the first time around — was a blur.

My decision was shriveling up in my brain.

"I should be quiet," Jeannie went on. "I'm being so negative."

"That's okay. Maybe you're right, Jeannie."

"No. I was wrong. You should do this, because you know yourself better than I do —"

"That's just it, Jeannie, I *don't* know! Everyone's been telling me what to do. And they're all right. I can't even think straight. And the worst thing is, I have to decide right away or it'll be too late! And I have so much on my mind. The Color War is starting in two days and we have a meeting tomorrow and I didn't even do my homework tonight and I have to call Joanna and Shira and Josh —"

"Don't worry, Claudia," Jeannie said gently. "I'll call the other three. We can all talk about it tomorrow. Just shut it all out. Do the homework. Relax. Listen to some music. Go to bed. Okay?"

"Yeah." My voice was cracking. Jeannie is such a good friend.

"Promise?"

"Promise."

Well, I did finish my homework, but I didn't listen to music. I didn't try Mark again either. I was too tired. I just conked right out.

The next morning I must have changed my mind a hundred times. Jeannie and Stacey had spread the news, so everyone knew now. And everyone had an opinion.

I was relieved to escape to homeroom.

Mark was late for school (which is not that unusual). As he slid into his seat, he smiled and whispered, "What's going on?"

Ms. Pilley was glowering at us. So I wrote him a note and handed it to him when she wasn't looking.

He read it carefully and wrote something back.

Stay, dear Claudia, or my life is over, he scribbled on a sheet stained with tears.

As if.

Actually, this is what his note said:

Cool. You get to graduate a year early & leav this dump.

Okay, so it wasn't romantic. Guys are programmed to hide their feelings. Everyone knows that.

Mark was hiding them pretty deeply as we walked to class after homeroom.

"So?" I said. "What do you think about the news?"

"What I want to know is, how did you do it? Did your parents pay off Amer?"

"Oooh, that's low, Jaffe. Very low." I began punching him on the arm. He ran off, laughing, but I caught up.

"Truce!" he yelled, shielding himself with his books.

"Aren't you upset?" I blurted out.

"No way. I was relieved. I thought you were sending me a note about the Color War meeting or something."

"Mark, I can't believe you! I'm, like, a nervous wreck about this. How will you feel if I decide to go back to eighth grade?"

Mark shrugged. "So? We'll still be in the same school."

Good point.

I smiled and took his arm.

Maybe I was taking this too seriously. Mark had the right attitude. Keep cool, no matter what.

I knew there was a reason I liked him.

CHAPTER 7

"Hey, queenie babes!" shouted Ron Tibbets from the other end of the gym. "How do you spell 'limerick'?"

I looked up from the SMS Color War banner I was helping to paint on the gym floor. "Queenie babes?"

"What a jerk," Shira said.

Josh rose to his feet. "I'll beat him up!"

Joanna nearly collapsed with laughter.

"Look it up!" I called back. *"And it's Claudia!"*

"Okay, Claudia babes!"

Sigh. I guess every class has an Alan Gray.

To be honest, in the back of my mind, I half wished *Mark* would beat him up. He might have offered, if he'd been there.

But he wasn't. And it was already twenty minutes into the biggest Color War meeting of the year.

Wednesday, after school, was the seventh-graders' time to decorate the gym (sixth grade had Tuesday and eighth had Thursday). We were putting up orange streamers, balloons, posters, the works. Josh, Shira, Joanna, Jeannie, and I were painting a humongous mural with a "war" theme, using our class color.

I looked at the door, hoping Mark would show up. He was supposed to be in charge of setting up a sound system. No one else seemed to know how. Mr. Kingbridge, our faculty adviser, had already brought in two sets of wires that didn't work.

I tried not to be angry with Mark. He can be pretty absentminded. But he *was* co-coordinator, and I had reminded him twice that day.

"It just doesn't make sense," Shira said, carefully painting an orange gladiator.

"Maybe he's at Frank's," I replied.

Shira peered up. "Who?"

"Mark."

"I was talking about *you*, going into eighth grade. Weren't you listening? It doesn't make sense that you're at the top of your class now, and you want to go back to the bottom."

"How do you know she'll be at the bottom?" Josh retorted.

"Eighth grade is hard," Joanna remarked.

"You guys have no faith," Josh said.

"Am I hearing right?" Shira asked. "You *want* her to go, Josh?"

"I didn't say that! It's just that, well, Claudia

should do what makes her happy." Josh quickly looked down at the orange Sherman tank he was painting. "I guess."

No one said anything for awhile. Then Jeannie sighed and sat back. Her eyes were kind of moist. "This feels so weird. I mean, here we are, painting all this seventh-grade Color War stuff, using your plans, Claudia, because you're our class Queen and all — and soon you may be in another grade!"

Glurp. I felt as if a big day-old Swedish meatball had lodged itself in my throat.

I did not want to talk about this now. Preparing for the Color War was stressful enough. "Look, guys, can we — ?"

"We'll really miss you if you go, Claudia," Joanna murmured softly.

"A lot," Shira added.

Josh's eyes darted toward me. He looked as if he were going to say something, but he didn't. He seemed deeply into his art.

Tears began to well up in my eyes. I blinked them back.

And then I saw Mark, coming through the gym door.

I put down my brush and ran.

"Hi! Where were you?" I called out.

"Sorry," he said with a sheepish smile. "Frank and me? We were having this big, heavy conversation about packing? And I started walking out of school with him. I'm halfway to his house and I slap myself on the head, like, 'What am I doing?' So I ran back." He rolled his eyes. "I know, I know, duh!"

What could I say? My anger was melting. "Come look at our mural." I held his hand and we walked across the room.

"Yo, Mark!" Shira blurted out. "Can't you talk some sense into her?"

"About what?" Mark asked.

"Not now, Shira," I pleaded.

"Tell her not to skip into eighth grade," Shira barreled on.

"We *know* she'll listen to you," Joanna added.

"Yeah, well, sure," Mark said with a shrug. "She should. If she wants. Definitely."

"Don't sound so upset," Josh muttered.

"Uh, guys? This is a meeting?" I reminded everyone. "Mark, can you help Mr. Kingbridge set up the speakers?"

Mark looked at his watch. "Sure. For about twenty minutes. Then I have to go. The O'Malleys are taking me to dinner."

He jogged away toward the sound system.

Josh looked as if he'd smelled something bad. *"The O'Malleys are taking him to dinner?"*

"He couldn't tell them no, for something like this?" Shira muttered.

"It's important," I explained. "Frank's moving. They've been friends for life. They have to, you know, bond."

"Why doesn't he just move with them?" Josh asked.

I threw a paint rag at him. "Get back to work, Rocker."

The meeting ended late. We straggled out of school, exhausted. I said a weary good-bye to my friends and headed home.

Unfortunately I had to walk fast. The BSC meeting would be starting in a few minutes.

A cold November wind made me button up my coat. Leaves were falling around me, but the gray sky seemed to dull their colors.

A perfect day for my mood. Gray.

I had thought the Color War meeting would be refreshing. I had thought it would take my mind off my Big Decision.

But it hadn't. I felt worse. Something else was creeping into my mind now. Something else that just didn't feel right in my life.

My relationship with Mark.

"I'll walk with you."

I jumped at the sudden sound of Josh's voice. "Don't scare me like that!"

"Walking home with me is scary?"

"You know what I mean. And thanks, but I'm kind of in a hurry. Anyway, how can you walk me? You live in totally the wrong direction."

Josh shrugged. "Depends on your definition of wrong. If I keep going, I'll get home anyway. Columbus proved it."

"You are weird, Rocker."

"Flattery will get you everywhere. Now, what's up? You look awful."

"Thanks a lot."

"No! Not *awful* awful — I mean, you look great. Just — awful in the *mood* sense. Like something's wrong. Like you could use a friend. That's all."

I couldn't help laughing. I love it when Josh becomes flustered. It brings out the sweetness in him.

And it sure felt nice that *someone* cared.

"Josh, have you ever felt your whole life turn upside down?" I asked.

"Sure." Josh nodded. "It was at this cool amusement park. The Cyclospin —"

I gave him a slap. "Can't you ever be —"

"Serious? Yeah." Josh took a deep breath. "Like when my grandfather was dying. He was living in our house. I couldn't do a thing about it. I felt upside down, inside out, you name it."

"Oh, Josh. You never told me this."

"You never asked," Josh said with a sad smile. "Anyway, I don't like talking about it. You know me. Hap-hap-happy. I have to really care a lot about somebody before I open up."

"You should talk to Mark."

"Mark?"

"Yeah. He just closes up when he cares about someone. At least that's the way he is with me. I mean, I figured it was a *guy* thing, but you're not like that. Why would *he* be?"

"Wait. You want to talk about Mark? That's why you're upset?"

I shrugged. "Yeah. Is that okay?"

"Sure! I just . . . assumed you wanted to talk about, you know, something more serious. The eighth-grade thing."

"This is serious too, Josh! Look, you've known Mark longer than I have. This is just his style, right? Being kind of cool and absent-minded? Should I be worried?"

"Well, I don't know. I mean, he's cool and absentminded to me, and I don't worry —"

"But he's more than that, Josh. He's kind and funny and — well, you wouldn't know. But I'm just not seeing that good stuff anymore. Maybe I'm not important to him. Even with this big decision of mine he says, 'Hey, we'll still be in the same school.' Which is true, but still. Shouldn't he show *some* emotion? I mean, he seems more interested in Frank."

"But Frank's moving, right? And —"

"Now *you're* making excuses for him. I am so sick and tired of excuses. Frank Frank Frank.

Frank's not his girlfriend. I am. And I may be moving too, just in a different way."

We were already in front of my house. I stopped and turned to face Josh. "I'm sorry. I'm yelling. And I've been talking your ear off."

"It's okay," Josh said. "Really."

I grabbed his hand. "You are such a good friend."

Josh blushed and looked suddenly downward. "Uh, Claudia . . ."

I glanced at my watch.

"Five twenty-eight?" I let go of Josh and ran toward the house. "Oh my lord. Kristy's going to kill me if I'm late. Thanks, Josh, you were a big help!"

"Wait . . . Claudia?" Josh called out in an urgent voice.

As I opened my front door, I looked over my shoulder. "What?"

All Josh said was, "Have a good meeting."

I thanked him, bolted inside, and shut the door.

CHAPTER 8

Our Wednesday meeting was a zoo. We stopped being the Baby-sitters Club. Instead, we were archrivals. The White, the Blue, and the Orange, at our last BSC meeting before the SMS Color War.

And we had fistfuls of junk food, which meant . . .

FOOOOOD FIIIIGHT!

I, the only orange member, was outnumbered but not outclassed. No matter how many rivals pelted me, I managed to eat their ammunition.

After the battle, Kristy told us her news: She'd talked her way into co-coordinating the eighth-grade festivities. Which meant she had to work shoulder-to-shoulder with her least favorite person in the world, the horrible and disgusting Alan Gray. (Alan, by the way, adores Kristy. He just has funny ways of showing it. Like picking his nose over her lunch tray.) Kristy insisted they were working fine together.

During lunch the following day, Thursday, I spotted Kristy chasing Alan through the hallway with a handful of wet papier-mâché.

That evening Stacey called me in hysterics (laughing, not crying). At the eighth-grade setup in the gym, Alan had "practiced" at the portrait booth by doing a likeness of Kristy that resembled a rat. Kristy broke it over his head.

Who needed a Color War? All we needed to do was watch those two.

As for us seventh-graders, well, we were hot. All day Thursday, my design committee was at work. Orange posters in the hallways. Plastic oranges hanging from the light fixtures. Orange streamers and balloons everywhere. And across the front hallway of our school, our class motto:

ORANGE YOU GLAD YOU'RE IN SEVENTH GRADE?

(No, I can't take credit. It was Josh's idea.)

I could barely sleep Thursday night. From total, utter, sheer excitement.

That was the best thing about the Color War. It was taking over my life. Making me forget about everything else. I was too involved to worry about Mark. Or my Big Decision.

It could all wait. The whole school had Color War fever. Even the teachers were going light on the homework.

And I, Claudia the Fashion Doctor, had actually found a cool orange outfit — right in my closet. It was an electric orange rayon bowling ensemble I'd bought at a flea market and almost forgotten about.

Friday was It. Day One of the Color War of the Century.

On the way to school, Stacey, Mary Anne, Mal, Jessi, and I could hear the buzz of excitement two blocks before we reached SMS.

"Oh my lord," Stacey said as the school came into sight.

We all stopped short and gaped.

Above the front door, hanging across the marble slab carved with our school's name, was an enormous blue banner.

It read EIGHTH GRADE RULES!

"This really is war," I murmured.

"Who put that there?" Jessi asked.

At that moment, Kristy emerged from the crowd, waving to us.

"Like it?" she shouted proudly.

Figures.

I don't know how she got permission. I don't know when she managed to put it up.

But I was mad.

"You ain't seen nothing yet," I said to her as I huffed into school.

I'm not sure what happened during the first half of the day. I was thinking about fourth period. That was the official time for the entire school to report to the gym.

I guess I should explain. Each day a different period had been designated for the festivities. This way, we'd only be giving up one class day in each subject. (On the last day — the big finale — Color War was to be held after school.)

When the fourth-period bell finally rang, I flew.

I sat with Mark in the bleachers. Jeannie, Shira, Joanna, and Josh sat behind us. "I am so-o-o-o-o excited!" I said, squeezing Mark's arm.

"WOOO! SEVENTH GRADE! YEAH!" he shouted.

The teachers managed to herd everybody off the gym floor, where the events had been set up. Mr. Kingbridge gave a long, boring speech over the megaphone, then introduced the events coordinators.

When he mentioned my name, the gym shook with the noise. Seriously. I guess it was because of my friends in all three grades.

For a moment I felt weird, seeing Stacey and the others in a different section of the bleachers. I felt as if I should be sitting with the eighth grade.

Then Kristy started leading a cheer of "BLUE RULES!"

And the sixth grade began chanting "FIGHT FOR WHITE!"

I knew just where I belonged at that moment.

"ORANGE YOU GLAD YOU'RE IN SEVENTH?" I shouted.

Everyone joined in, until Mr. Kingbridge quieted us down and announced, "Friday events, begin!"

My event was the portrait booth. Alan and a sixth-grader named Nicole were the other teams' artists. Bonnie Lasher was sitting for the portrait.

"Give up now, Kishi," Alan said in his goony voice.

I grabbed a tan-colored Craypa. It stuck to my hand.

Bubble gum.

Alan was trying very hard not to giggle.

"You rotten, stinking —" I stood up. Alan took off like a shot.

Calmly I scrawled a message on his wooden stool in thick black Craypa:

!ƎM ʞƆIʞ

And then I went to work.

Alan managed to slither back. I made sure to keep eye contact while he sat down.

I have to say, I did a fabulous likeness of Bonnie. She loved it. So did Mr. Kingbridge.

"One point for Orange!" he shouted through the megaphone.

"Lucky," Alan said.

What a sore loser.

He became even sorer later on, when kids began kicking him for no reason. (Well, no reason *he* could figure out. Heh-heh.)

The other events? Well, the sixth-graders narrowly won the bake-off. The highlight was Jessi's chocolate mousse fudge cake surprise.

The eighth-graders won the instant limerick contest. My favorite was written by Emily Bernstein, on the topic of "nightmares."

> There once was a fellow named Ed,
> Who had a bad nightmare in bed.
> He twisted and wrangled;
> His pj's got tangled,
> And he woke with his pants on his head.

The period flew by. By the end, the score was White 8, Blue 8, and Orange 7.

I admit, I was feeling down.

But definitely not out.

I looked around for Mark. I wanted to walk with him to lunch, but the crowd was pushing me out the gym door, shoulder-to-shoulder with Jeannie.

We made our way down the corridor toward

the cafeteria. Joanna was right behind us, with Shira and Josh.

"Bad start," Joanna grumbled.

"We still have five days," I said.

"We're underdogs," Josh added. "The world loves an underdog."

"Oh? Then *you* should be King of the Seventh Grade," Shira remarked.

"You die, Epstein!"

Josh took off after her. The two of them ran through the crowd, shouting and laughing.

"They never stop, do they?" I asked.

"They've been that way for years," Jeannie replied.

Just then something occurred to me. Something that seemed so obvious I should have thought of it long ago. "Do you think he . . . *likes* her?"

Jeannie looked puzzled. "Who, Shira?"

"Yeah. I can't believe I never saw this. The other day Josh walked me home from school. I mean, he lives all the way on Centennial Avenue, right? So there had to be a reason. Anyway, he was acting kind of strange, telling me personal things. . . ."

"What does this have to do with Shira?"

"He seemed to want to say something, but he kind of clammed up. You know Josh. If it's not a joke, his tongue goes into knots. Maybe he wanted advice. *Love* advice."

Jeannie was giving me an odd look. "Maybe. But I don't think this is about Shira."

"No?"

"Claudia, don't you . . . ? Oh, never mind."

"What? Don't I *what*?" I gave Jeannie a Look. "Uh-oh. Something's up. Gossip meter, gossip meter!"

"Nothing . . ."

"Oh, no, you don't. You're committed now. You have to tell me."

Jeannie exhaled deeply. "Well . . . it's you, Claudia."

"What's me?"

"Who Josh needs the advice about. Josh likes *you*."

"Ha-ha. Very funny. I know he likes me. I mean, as a friend."

Jeannie rolled her eyes. "Claudia, *duh*, when are you going to figure this out? He only drops what he's doing every time you're near. He follows you around school all the time. His main goal in life is to make you laugh."

"But that's his personality, Jeannie!" I could not believe I was having this conversation. I laughed aloud. "You are dreaming. Look, I can tell when boys like me, and Josh doesn't *like* me that way."

"If you say so."

"Well, what makes you so sure? Has he talked to you about this?"

"He doesn't need to. Don't you see his face whenever Mark is near? It crumbles up like a leaf. Can't you hear how he quiets down and kind of shrinks away?"

"No!"

"That's because you're busy looking at Mark. Ask anyone, Claudia. You're the only one who doesn't know."

I turned toward Joanna. "Are you hearing this?"

Joanna nodded. "It's true, Claudia."

Oh, please.

This was not happening.

For a moment I allowed myself to imagine this being true. I tried to take the theory seriously.

I couldn't. It cracked me up.

No. Absolutely not.

"You're both crazy," I said as we turned into the cafeteria.

CHAPTER 9

Saturday

Today was Day 2 of the
Kid's Color War. Kristy
brought over the Papadakises
and I baby-sat for the
Arnold twins. A group of
parents helped out. We
had a fun time.

Fun? It was sensational. The
kids loved it.

Well, at the beginning
there were a few rough
spots. You have to admit
that, Kristy.

Okay, Jackie Rodowsky's, um,
butt is a little sore. But that was
his fault...

"Listen up, warriors!" Kristy announced to the crowd of kids on Brenner Field. "Mary Anne will take the Leaf-Raking Contest. Mallory will do Speed Checkers. Home Run Derby contestants, follow me!"

"YEEEAAAAA!"

By Saturday, the Kids' Color War had been completely Kristyfied. The kids were evenly divided into three teams — red, green, and black — each calculated to have the same average age. All the events had been planned in advance.

A few parents were on hand to help, including a doctor (Charlotte Johanssen's mom).

As the Home Run Derby contestants followed Kristy, she pointed to the outfield. On it, she'd used chalk powder to make long, thick lines in semicircles at different distances from the plate. "Those are the home run lines," Kristy explained. "The closest for the youngest kids, the farthest for the oldest. Now, this is not a softball game. No baserunning. No outs. Each person gets three chances to hit a home run. The team with the most home runs wins."

She took a scorecard out of her pocket and read off names. In minutes, half the kids were lined up to bat and half were in the outfield (to retrieve batted balls).

"Ba-a-a-a-atter up!" Kristy shouted.

Adam Pike, a red-team member, stepped up to home plate. He swung his bat fiercely (he is *very* competitive).

Jackie Rodowsky, who was on the black team, pounded his mitt in short center field. "Bat 'em, Adam!" he shouted.

"Ha-ha, so funny I forgot to laugh," Adam said.

Kristy wound up for the pitch.

"*Madam*, there's *Adam*, he's going to *bat 'em*," Jackie recited. "So don't *pat 'im*."

Jackie began giggling hysterically at his own joke. He twisted and fell to the ground on all fours.

SMMMMACK! went Adam's bat as he made contact with the ball.

Have I mentioned that Jackie's nickname is the Walking Disaster?

Thump.

Kristy actually heard the ball thud against Jackie's rear end.

"Interference!" cried Adam.

"YEEEEOOOOOWWW!" cried Jackie.

"That would have been a home run if he hadn't stuck himself in the way!" Adam insisted.

Dr. Johanssen raced over to Jackie. So did most of the other players (the ones who weren't laughing like crazy).

PHWEEEEEET! went Kristy's referee's whistle. "Give the patient some air!"

Dr. Johanssen knelt over Jackie. "Where were you hit? Will you show me?"

Jackie turned beet-red. Now everyone was cracking up. Even Kristy.

Across the field, Mary Anne's teams were busy raking. Mary Anne had divided a leaf-covered patch of grass into three long lanes. The object: to be the fastest to leave your lane of grass totally leafless. Six kids were involved, two on a team.

Vanessa Pike and Madeleine DeWitt were green-team partners. Vanessa's nine, but Madeleine is only four. She didn't quite understand the process. She was raking leaves *into* the lane.

"Mary *A-a-a-anne!*" Vanessa shouted. "Madeleine's just making it worse! I call a time-out!"

"No fair!" cried Carolyn Arnold from the red team's lane. "No time-outs allowed!"

"We're winning!" shouted a gleeful Patsy Kuhn from the black lane.

Mary Anne absolutely hates confrontations. "Well, um —"

"Sto-o-op!" shouted Patsy's sister (and black-team partner), Laurel. "Charlotte's sabotouching my rake!"

Charlotte, who was the other red-team member, had gotten her metal rake tangled up in

77

Laurel's. The two girls were yanking and yanking, but it only seemed to make things worse.

Mary Anne took a deep breath and shouted, "TIME-OUT!"

As Charlotte and Laurel straightened things out, Mary Anne gave Madeleine a raking lesson.

Linny was watching them from the edge of right field. (He, of course, was in the Home Run Derby.) "That is the dumbest competition," he commented.

Vanessa stuck her tongue out at him. "You just missed a fly ball."

It was true. Linny looked up helplessly at a softball sailing over his head.

A softball hit by Jackie Rodowsky.

Now, even I know that Jackie is a terrible softball player. The bruise must have given him special athletic abilities. "I did it! I did it!" he shrieked happily.

In a fit of glee, he threw his bat in the air. It sailed toward the Speed Checkers players.

"Jackie, no-o-o-o-o-o!" shouted Kristy and Mary Anne at the same time.

"Duck!" warned Mallory.

Players dived out of the way. The bat crashed down on a game of checkers. Pieces scattered over the grass. Mrs. Pike, who was helping out, almost had a heart attack.

Kristy and Mary Anne both ran to the scene.

Hannie burst into tears.

"Are you all right?" Mary Anne asked. "Did the bat hit you?"

"No!" she wailed. "But look at the game! I was winning!"

"He almost killed me!" screamed Margo Pike.

"Jackie, you should know better," Kristy scolded. "That violated Krushers rule number one."

"Sorry," Jackie said sheepishly.

"Don't worry, we'll start the game over," Mallory reassured Hannie.

"But that's not fair!" Hannie said. "It should count as an automatic win!"

"YEAH! NO FAIR!" bellowed Linny, who was storming in to defend his sister. "And she *never* wins because she's such a stinky player, so this means a lot."

"I am not stinky!" Hannie retorted.

"Guys . . ." Kristy said.

From the Leaf-Raking Contest, Laurel's voice rang out. "Your team did *not* win, Vanessa! Mary Anne wasn't here, so it's a do-over!"

"Do-over? Who's going to put the leaves back?" Vanessa shouted.

"Be right there!" Mary Anne called out.

"Come on, pitcher, my turn to bat!" yelled Byron Pike.

"I'm bored!" announced Jake Kuhn from the outfield.

"I quit!" declared Hannie.

"Is there a bathroom nearby?" Marilyn Arnold asked.

PHWEEEEEEET!

Kristy's whistle pierced the air. "All teams report to me! Time for a pep talk!"

"Pep talk?" Byron groaned. "That'll ruin my rhythm!"

Sniffling, moaning, complaining, the kids all slumped toward Kristy.

With a sigh, Kristy gave Mary Anne a weary Look. "Whose idea was this anyway?" she muttered.

"Yours, I think," Mary Anne said gently.

CHAPTER 10

Two hands closed over my eyes. "Do no-o-ot even attempt to mo-o-o-ve!" rasped a deep voice behind me.

"Hi, Mark," I said. "Can you give me a neck rub?"

"How did you know it was me?"

I smiled and looked over my shoulder. "You're wearing the Escape cologne I bought you for your birthday."

Mark was standing one step above me in the bleachers. It was Monday, and we were about to begin Day Two of the SMS Color War.

I was happy to see him. Despite the tough weekend.

What had I done since Friday? Think, argue, and cry.

I thought a lot about my Big Decision. And about why Mark was acting so weird. And about why Jeannie was so convinced Josh liked me.

I argued with my mom and dad when they bugged me about my choice for the hundredth time (after insisting they would "give me space").

I cried after Mark called to cancel our Saturday night date. (No, he didn't cancel because of Frank this time. His dad needed help buying an outboard motor or something.)

Boy, was I angry. I actually said to him, "It's me or the boat, take your choice!"

He went with his dad. But he did call later on, and he came over to my house on Sunday. And he actually rescheduled our date — for Monday after school. Plus, he put up with my crabby mood. So I forgave him.

Now, on Monday, I was feeling exhausted. I still hadn't made my decision. I'd been up practically all night again. In the morning I woke up in a daze. I couldn't even dress myself properly. Without thinking, I slipped on a pair of orange-striped harem pants and a dark blue blouse.

Half blue. Half orange. It made sense, in a way. It described my state of mind.

Don't worry, I changed blouses. Now I was all orange.

And for the first time, I was beginning to feel human — thanks to Mark's neck massage.

"Whoa, this is like a rock," Mark said. "Tense, huh?"

"Yeah. But that feels good."

"Still worried about what grade to go into?"

"Yup."

"You take a long time to make decisions. Me? I just go with the first thing that pops into my mind. I figure, hey, just do it."

"It's not that simple! This isn't like trying to decide whether to watch basketball or football on TV!"

"I didn't say that —"

"Well, what are you saying, Mark?"

Mark's hands let go of my neck. "Look, Claudia, I was just talking, that's all. I mean, if you want me to shut up, I will."

Easy, Claudia, I told myself. *He's concerned. He's giving you a neck rub. What more do you want?*

I turned around. "I'm sorry. I — I hardly slept last night."

"That's okay," Mark said. "Oh. I almost forgot. Listen, could you — ?"

"Will today's three-legged-race contestants please take your places?" Mr. Kingbridge's voice blared over the speakers.

Oops. That included me.

"Hold that thought! See you later!" I stood up and ran onto the floor.

My partner was Josh. Josh, the boy I supposedly didn't really know. My mystery lover.

Puh-leeze.

I was not, *not* going to lose this race to a fit of giggles.

Josh was waiting behind the starting line, pulling something from his pocket.

With a flourish, he unfolded a large silk handkerchief. Printed on it was a famous abstract painting by the artist Joan Miró.

"Like it?" Josh asked.

"It's upside down," I said.

"Oh. Sure. I knew that. I was just testing you." He grinned. His face flushed and he averted his eyes. "I knew Miró was one of your favorites. . . ."

Hmmm.

Okay. Okay. I had to think about this.

How did Josh know I liked Miró? Even Stacey didn't know that.

Had I told him? I must have.

But he actually remembered? That was the kind of thing that would pass through Mark's head like wind through a picket fence.

And where on earth did he find the scarf? Guys don't have things like that. Did he buy it? Smuggle it from his mom's collection?

Just because of me?

Was it possible?

Josh . . . me?

Josh was twisting the scarf into a tight cord. "Uh, Earth to Claudia? Our race?"

"Oh. Right."

Okay. Calm down. Be real.

He was Josh. The scarf was just typical . . . Joshness. This was a race. We were partners. No more. No less. No problem.

I was overthinking. I was stressed.

"So," Josh said, "uh, should we, you know . . . tie this?"

He was sweating. His face was pink and his hands were shaky. He'd put his leg next to mine — about an inch away, though. As if he were afraid to touch.

He's a boy. Boys are like that.

"Sure, Josh."

I touched my ankle to his. Josh tried to tie a knot, but his fingers kept slipping.

The other three-legged contestants were waiting for us. Already some of the other events had started. Mr. Kingbridge was walking toward us now, looking concerned.

Quickly I took the scarf from Josh. "I'll tie it."

For a moment, our fingers touched. As I started tying, I glanced up at him.

That was when I saw it.

It only lasted a moment. A split second. But I caught him looking at me when he thought I wasn't looking.

It's hard to explain. He wasn't drooling or ogling or anything. Just looking. But I'd never seen his eyes quite that way. If they had been hands, they would have been holding me gently, the way you hold a flower. If they had been a blanket, they would have been covering me to protect against the cold.

No boy had ever looked at me like that. Ever. Not even Mark.

Then — *pffft* — the look was gone. Josh glanced away instantly.

But that was enough.

I knew. Just like that.

Jeannie was right.

Images of Josh flooded into my mind. The awkward conversations. The constant jokes. The smiles. The little gifts. The walks home. My friends' comments that were really, all along, hints.

You're the only one who doesn't know. Jeannie's words came back to me.

How could I have been so stupid?

My poor, knotted stomach gave one more twist.

I swallowed hard.

"Claudia?" Mr. Kingbridge said.

The contest. We were in a contest.

"Oh!" I said. "We're ready."

Josh's left arm and my right were squashed against our sides. Josh looked at my shoulder questioningly.

I couldn't help laughing. "It's not dusty. Go ahead."

To reassure him, I put my arm around his shoulder. He did the same to me.

He smiled. I smiled.

"On your mark . . ." Mr. Kingbridge announced.

We stepped to the line.

"Get set . . ."

We bent our knees together.

I had a ridiculous thought. I imagined us as boyfriend and girlfriend. Josh and me.

The thought nearly made me scream with laughter.

Silly. Totally silly.

"GO!"

Josh lifted his leg. My leg tightened in response. I felt off balance. My body slipped downward.

The blue team had shot ahead of us.

"Come on!" Josh said, gripping me tighter.

I don't know how I stayed upright. But I did.

"Okay, *step*!" I grunted.

We stumbled on the next step. But our third step was clean. And our fourth. We were hitting a rhythm. Lifting our tied-together legs at the same time now. Taking faster steps. Clutching each other's shoulders for support.

The white-team couple beside us fell, almost knocking into Josh. We ignored them.

Now the blue-team partners were starting to crack up. That slowed them down.

"Step!" Josh yelled.

We both lengthened our strides. We were practically leaping.

The blue team was bumbling toward the finish line. Then one of them turned to look at us.

Big mistake. They hit the floor in a heap.

With a grunt, Josh and I hurled ourselves over the line.

"Yyyyyyyessss!" Josh shouted.

And *then* we fell.

We were giggling hysterically. My free leg was tangled with his. Our arms were pinned against the floor.

I hoisted myself up and swung around, trying to sit up. I kind of fell over Josh.

We were face-to-face. Josh stopped laughing. So did I.

Kiss him.

Where did that thought come from?

I shut it out.

Way out.

"Uh, Claudia?" Josh said softly.

Oh, boy. This was it. The Moment. Josh pouring out his heart. Right here on the gym floor.

"Yes?" I asked.

"Your elbow is in my kidney. Could you sit up?"

"Oh! Sorry!"

I pushed myself off of him. I untied the scarf, and we both stood up.

The seventh-grade section of the bleachers was screaming at us. Cheering like crazy.

Josh grabbed my hand and we raised our arms in victory.

"Let's clear out for the next teams," Mr. Kingbridge said to us.

I gave Josh's hand a quick squeeze, and we ran off.

Right into Mark.

He was standing at the base of the bleachers. "You guys looked good," he said.

"Josh did it," I replied. "He had to pull me along."

I looked at Josh. He nodded and smiled tightly. "Yeah. Well. I'll, uh, see you."

"Where are you —"

But he was gone. Jogging toward the water cooler.

I was alone with Mark.

My head was reeling. I was uncomfortable. Nervous. Embarrassed, a little.

As if Mark had caught me with another guy.

He had, of course. But the other guy was just Josh. And *he* was the one who liked *me*, not vice versa.

So why was I feeling so weird?

"How's the neck?" Mark asked.

"Fine! Just great!" My voice was too loud. Too cheerful. "Great race, huh?"

"Yup." Mark nodded and looked away. "Uh, Claudia? Getting back to what we were talking about . . ."

"Now?" I groaned. "Let's not. I'll make a decision today or tomorrow."

"I wasn't talking about that. It's just that — well, remember when I started to tell you something, right before the events?"

"Yeah . . ." I lied.

"Okay, what I was going to say was, you know how we were going to go out after school?"

"You can't go." I meant it as a question, but it came out like a statement.

"Not today. But maybe tomorrow?"

I lost it. I wanted to smack him. "That's the third time, Mark!"

"Not really. I came over Sunday."

"That wasn't a *date* date —"

"Yeah, okay, I'm sorry and all, but my brother? His friend is coming over, and they need to —"

"It's fine, Mark," I interrupted him. "Whatever. Call me later."

Or never.

I didn't care.

I stormed away.

CHAPTER 11

"Christmas shopping," said Stacey. "That's what we need to do."

Cute. Josh was cute. But was he boyfriend cute?

"Claudia?"

Mark was boyfriend cute. Josh was more like stuffed-animal cute.

"Claudia? Did you hear me?"

Wake up, Kishi!

"Sorry," I said. "I heard you."

We were turning the corner into the SMS lobby. Monday's classes had just ended, and kids were racing all around us. The Color War period had been over hours ago, but I was still thinking about my race with Josh.

What did it mean? I had no idea. For one thing, I hadn't talked to Josh the rest of the day. He'd been avoiding me.

I think he wanted to talk to me after school, when we were at our lockers. But something got in the way.

Mark.

He'd been avoiding me too. But since our lockers were so close, we absolutely *had* to see each other. And what did he do then? Did he try to comfort me? Did he apologize for breaking off our date? No, he just mumbled that excuse about his brother again. He promised to call, and then he took off.

Josh, who had been at his locker during this time, turned and left.

Thank goodness I ran into Stacey. It was nice to be around someone I didn't feel hopelessly confused about.

"Anyway, we have enough time to go downtown before the BSC meeting —" Stacey was saying.

"Wait a minute," I interrupted her. "Did you say Christmas shopping? *Today?*"

"Sure."

"Stacey, the *Thanksgiving* decorations just went up!"

"Yes, but we have to face facts. Only forty-five more shopping days, including weekends. Which may sound like a lot, but think about it. At least thirty of them are school days, plus baby-sitting on weekends, plus parties and family stuff —"

"Stacey, we don't have time —"

"We'll just window-shop. Check out the

sales at Bellair's." Stacey sighed. "Look, Claudia, you need this. You're not yourself. This grade thing is getting to you. You need to unwind. Think about it: You and me, hanging out, looking at clothes —"

"Eating —"

"Making up stories about the shoppers —"

"The fashion victims —"

Stacey laughed. "Just like the old days!"

The old days.

The days before I was sent back. When my personal life was uncomplicated. When I was in the same grade, the same classes, with my very best friend.

"Claudia?" Mrs. Amer's voice interrupted my thoughts.

Yikes.

I turned. Mrs. Amer was standing just to my right, in the guidance office hallway. "May I speak with you a moment?" she asked.

What now?

"I'll wait for you outside the front door," Stacey whispered.

I followed Mrs. Amer down the corridor. She stopped outside the office, far away from the crowd in the main hallway.

"I just wanted to remind you about our meeting with your parents on Friday," she said softly.

"Right," I said. "I know."

"Have you been giving the matter much thought?"

Just about twenty zillion hours, I wanted to say. "Sure," I replied. "But I haven't decided."

"That's perfectly all right, for now. But I would like to have this settled by the end of the conference, if not before. For *your* sake, dear."

"Okay. Thanks."

We said good-bye, and I quickly left the school.

Stacey was out front. "Well?" she asked.

"Just reminding me," I grumped. "As if I needed it."

We began heading downtown.

"It must be so hard for you," Stacey said. "When I put myself in your shoes, I think, 'Hey? Why switch?' I mean, with your good grades and your boyfriend and all —"

"Right. My boyfriend who never wants to go out with me. He postponed again."

"Uh-oh. Well, in that case, look at it this way: You could dump him easier if you switched grades."

"Stacey, don't confuse me!"

"I'm not trying to!"

"Right. First you say I should stay in seventh grade —"

"I did not. I only said I could understand

how you feel. *I* would switch. I mean, if it were me. But it's not, so I'll shut up."

"Stacey, if I do switch, forget about Christmas vacation. Forget about parties and stuff. I'll be working all the time. I'll be a hermit until June."

"Another reason to do our shopping early." Stacey laughed. "Look, of course it wouldn't be easy. But you know we'd all help you after school. We could form, like, a think tank. And we'd be in classes together again, and — and that's all I have to say. I told myself I would not stress you out."

"It's okay, Stacey," I assured her.

"Claudia, we know you can do it. If you want to. But we also know you'll make the right decision for yourself — and either way, we're on your side."

"You know what my life is like now?" I asked. "Remember last summer, when we tried to build that great sand castle? And just when it was perfect, a wave would knock it down because the tide was coming in? *That's* what it's like. I think I've figured things out, I know exactly what to do — then something else happens to me. A conversation, a thought. And everything in my brain just falls apart."

Stacey nodded. "You have a lot on your mind. The Color War. Your boyfriend who's acting like a jerk. Baby-sitting —"

"Why couldn't Mrs. Amer just have *forced* me to switch back to eighth? Then I'd have to do it. I wouldn't be going through all this."

"Claudia, don't you see? She trusts you to make the decision. She wants you to be happy with it."

"But I'm miserable!"

"Well, I say there's only one answer."

"What?"

"Shop."

I smiled.

I am so lucky. Stacey understands me. She knows just what to say.

If only she knew *everything*.

If only I could tell her about Josh.

I desperately wanted to. But the words wouldn't come out. Somehow it didn't feel right.

What if I were wrong about him? I still didn't *know* he liked me. He hadn't told me so.

And what if I were right? What if Josh did have a huge crush on me? Should I talk about him behind his back, before he had the chance to confess?

It wouldn't be fair. I needed to talk to Josh first.

So I stayed quiet.

Stacey, by the way, was absolutely right. About the window-shopping, that is. It was just what I needed.

Well, it wasn't exactly window-shopping. Stacey bought a half-price, slinky black knit dress with a smocked tank top over a flowing calf-length skirt. I picked up a few headbands and barrettes, a pair of earrings, some candy and cookies, and the coolest orange vest I ever saw.

We walked home with five heavy shopping bags. We had to stop and rest every block.

It did feel like the old days.

Absolutely great.

We finally reached my bedroom at 5:24. Kristy was already there, scribbling on her clipboard.

"Uh, thanks, but my birthday was in August," she remarked.

"We were Christmas shopping," Stacey explained. "Sort of."

"*Now*?" Kristy asked. "Who'd you buy for?"

"Well, ourselves, actually," I replied.

Kristy howled with laughter. "Figures!"

I pulled a bag of Heath Bars out of my pack. "Here's a riddle. It's white, swims, has webbed feet, and quacks. It's a —?"

"Duck!" Kristy answered.

I threw the bag at her. "Don't say you weren't warned."

Kristy ducked. The candy landed in an open bag of plaster of paris.

As the other BSC members arrived, Kristy

and I were washing off Heath Bars in the bathroom sink, laughing like hyenas.

That set the tone for the rest of the BSC meeting. Everyone was feeling crazy. I'm not sure why. Maybe my good mood was rubbing off.

Between phone calls, we talked about the day's Color War contests. Abby reenacted *her* three-legged race with a boy named Alexander (she had dragged him, on his back, over the line). Kristy charmed us with her hog call, which had won the contest hands down. And Jessi tried to teach us the choreography of the routine she was preparing for the upcoming Color War group dance contest.

We barely had time to finalize our plans for the last day of the BSC Kids' Color War, which was to be Tuesday.

The meeting flew by. When it was over and everyone had gone, I flung myself onto my bed.

Dingdong! chimed the front doorbell.

Who could that be?

No one I was expecting. I mean, this was when Mark was supposed to have shown up, but —

I practically leaped off the bed. "I'll get it!"

Maybe his brother hadn't needed help after all. Maybe Mark had been kidding about canceling. He was surprising me.

I ran downstairs and pulled open the front door.

My uncle Russ was standing on the porch, grinning. "Hi, Claudia."

"Oh. Uncle Russ."

"Don't sound so happy."

Behind him I could see my aunt Peaches walking up the porch steps. She was holding my little cousin, the cutest baby in the world.

"Lynn!" I screamed, running past Uncle Russ. "Ooh, let me hold you!"

"We thought we'd stop by and surprise you," Peaches said.

"Lynn kept asking about you," Russ added. "She threatened to run away from home if we didn't come over right now."

I took Lynn from Peaches. She was fast asleep. I gave her about eighteen kisses, then I made sure to kiss Russ and Peaches.

I love my aunt and uncle. They are so cool that you forget they're grown-ups. Peaches is my mom's younger sister, but sometimes it feels as if she's my older sister. (Yes, Peaches is a nickname. Her real name is Miyoshi.)

My mom and dad had appeared and were chattering away with Russ. Peaches and I took Lynn into a little room in the back of our house. It used to be a playroom for Janine and me, but now it's set up with a crib, a rocking chair, and baby stuff.

I took Lynn's coat off and laid her gently in the crib. "She's so big," I whispered.

"Ten days is a long time in a baby's life," Peaches said, settling herself into the rocker.

"Was that how long ago I last saw her?"

Peaches nodded. "I understand a lot has happened in your life since then."

I sat on the carpet next to her. "Yeah, it's a total mess. Mom told you about it?"

"A little. She told me I shouldn't pester you, though."

"You're allowed. You and Stacey. She thinks I can handle eighth grade."

"Can you?"

"Maybe. But it's not so simple. I have friends in seventh grade. And my phantom boyfriend, Mark, who keeps standing me up."

"How dare he do that to my niece? He should be thrilled you even look at him!"

I laughed. "Yeah. Like Josh."

Peaches arched an eyebrow wa-a-a-a-ay up. "Oh? There are now *two* boys in your life?"

"No! I mean, I don't know yet. I mean, Josh is a boy. And he's in my life. But it's different. I think. I mean, I'm pretty sure *he* likes *me*."

"Uh-huh. And you? Do you like him?"

"Peaches, *Mark* is my boyfriend! Josh is . . . oh, I don't know. It's so complicated!"

Peaches nodded knowingly. "I know."

"You do? Has anything like this ever happened to you?"

Peaches just smiled. "Claudia, if I ask you something, will you promise to answer honestly?"

"Sure."

"How do *you* feel? Do you really care about Mark?"

I thought about it. Hard. It wasn't such an easy question. "I'm not sure anymore."

"Okay, then, put that aside. Separate question: Do you care about Josh?"

"Definitely. He's one of my best friends."

"Just a *friend*? That's all he is?"

I caught the "Yes" before it escaped from my mouth. *Yes* was not exactly the truth.

Which surprised even me.

"I don't know, Peaches," I said. "Maybe not."

CHAPTER 12

I learned a new word on Tuesday evening.

Pariah.

Janine taught it to me. It means "a person shunned by others." She called me "Claudia the Pariah."

She wasn't being mean. We had been talking about my day at school. And she'd thought of the perfect way to describe it.

All day long, my seventh-grade friends had shunned me.

Josh was acting as if I had some awful contagious disease. When I'd arrived at my locker before school, he was already off to his homeroom. In the cafeteria during lunch, he'd headed away from my table.

Even during the Color War, when our team had pulled into first place by four points and everybody was screaming and hugging each other, Josh had stayed far away.

That alone wouldn't have bothered me too

much. I figured, okay, he's embarrassed to talk to me. Tongue-tied. But the weirdest thing was that Shira, Joanna, and Jeannie had avoided me too.

I could guess what had happened. They must have talked to Josh. They must have known that Josh knew that I knew that Josh liked me. And they had been waiting for me to take the next step.

How did this become so complicated?

There were two bright spots. As I mentioned our team had pulled into the Color War lead that day. And Mark had apologized to me sweetly. He'd even asked me out after school — and had given me a signed guarantee that he'd show up.

To be honest, I was nervous about going out with him. So much had been happening. I didn't know how I felt about a lot of things anymore.

Especially about him.

As I approached my locker at the end of the day, Joanna, Jeannie, and Shira were huddled around Josh.

"Hi, guys!" I greeted them.

"We were just going," Shira said. " 'Bye, Claudia."

Off they flew.

All except for Josh. He was still stuffing books in his pack, looking very stiff.

"Hi, Josh!" I said as I pulled open my locker. "Can you believe it? We're ahead."

"Cool," Josh replied. "It's so cool. I mean, it's just really . . ."

"Cool?"

Josh burst out laughing. "I've been working on my vocabulary."

That was when I noticed his smile. I mean, *really* noticed it. And it was so contagious. It made his face very handsome.

Well, *more* handsome. He was pretty good-looking to begin with.

Could it work? Could I possibly . . . ?

Stop it, Claudia!

I guess Josh must have been reading my thoughts. When he glanced at me, he clammed right up.

"Well. I have all my books now," he said, backing down the hallway. "So, uh, 'bye."

He jogged away, then disappeared around the corner.

Claudia the Pariah strikes again.

As I finished loading up, I heard whispers. They were coming from around the corner Josh had just turned.

They were frantic, scolding whispers. And they were unmistakably the voices of Shira, Joanna, and Jeannie.

They'd been waiting for him!

His coaches. That's what they were.

They were planning strategy. Tactics. Whatever.

About *me*!

Why couldn't Josh just talk to me? Why was he being so immature?

Because he's a year younger, I reminded myself. He's supposed to be less mature. *I* was less mature a year ago.

Wasn't I?

It made sense that I was attracted to Mark. He's thirteen.

Not that he's the world's most mature person. But at least he's not tongue-tied and nervous. At least he knows what to say to me.

Even if it's not what I want to hear.

I looked around for him. He should have been here by now.

The hallway was emptying. Locker doors were slamming left and right.

I waited. I sat on the floor, leaning against the lower vents of my locker door. I tried to do some homework, but I couldn't concentrate.

When my back started aching, I stood up and walked to the front lobby.

Mark was leaning against the wall, near the glass display case. Jennifer Blye was with him, yakking away.

Jennifer has the world's worst crush on Mark. If I decided to switch grades, she would probably organize a victory parade.

"Mark?" I said, trying to sound nonchalant.

Mark turned. "Oh, hi, Claudia."

Jennifer's big, gooey smile vanished.

"I'm ready," I said patiently. "Are you?"

"Sure," Mark replied.

"Where are you guys going?" Jennifer asked.

"Yes, where are we going, Mark?" I asked.

"Uh . . . downtown, I guess," Mark said.

"That's where I'm going," Jennifer piped up.

I nudged Mark in the ribs. "Well," he said, "this is kind of a, you know . . ."

"Date," I added.

Jennifer huffed away. Mark and I left the school.

As we walked across the street, I could not keep my cool any longer. "You're forgiven," I snapped.

"Forgiven for what?" Mark said.

"I thought I heard you say, 'I'm sorry, Claudia.' Hmmm, maybe I just *assumed* you did, because it's the decent thing to do."

"Sorry for what? *She* was talking to *me*."

"Sorry for forgetting you were supposed to meet me, Mark!"

"I didn't!" Mark protested. "I was waiting."

"So was I — by my locker, where we always meet after school."

"I didn't need to go to my locker today!"

"I was supposed to know that? You could have come to meet me."

106

"Okay, okay —"

"Or at least apologized —"

"I'm sorry. All right?"

I didn't reply.

Our footsteps clacked dully as we headed toward the short route to town, through Brenner Field.

Mark was scowling. He looked as if he were heading to the dentist.

Some date.

I'd been looking forward to this for days. But now that we were finally together, I felt awful.

What was the point?

"Mark," I finally said. "Do you think this is working?"

"Do I think what is working?"

"*Us.*"

Mark shrugged. "I guess. I haven't thought about it that way."

That wasn't the answer I was hoping for. "What *do* you think about, Mark? Do you ever think about us?"

"Well . . . yeah. I am now, right? I mean, how can I help it?"

"I don't mean *now*! I mean, in general. It's just that, well, sometimes it seems as if you're . . . not there."

"So you're talking about yesterday and the day before? I *couldn't* be there. I had to postpone —"

"I don't mean *there* there. I mean *mentally* there. There for me."

"I don't get it, Claudia. Are you asking, like, are you my girlfriend? Because, yeah, that's what I tell people and all."

"I don't care what you tell people. I care about what you feel!"

"I don't know," Mark said. "I mean, how do *you* feel?"

Arrgh. This conversation was driving me crazy.

But it was a fair question. It deserved an honest answer.

"Right now?" I said. "I don't know how I feel about you, Mark. I don't think we're working out."

Mark exhaled loudly. We were walking on a dirt path through a grove of maple trees. Leaves were falling around us, and I caught a distant smoky whiff of someone's chimney.

"Claudia," Mark finally said, "is it another guy?"

That question took me by surprise. As far as I'd been concerned, this conversation had had two parts only: Mark and me.

But maybe I was wrong. Like it or not, Josh was in the picture. Exactly how, I wasn't sure. He wasn't the reason Mark and I were fighting. But maybe he was part of it.

Maybe I was seeing Mark more clearly because I knew someone else really cared about me.

"I don't know," I said softly.

We stopped near the opposite side of Brenner Field. Mark turned to me. His face was scrunched up in a frown.

I felt bad. Part of me wanted to reach out and hug him and tell him everything was all right.

But it wasn't. So much had been happening. The last few days had been rough for me. I'd been leaning on my family and my friends, dragging them through my dilemma. Stacey had been there for me. And my mom. And Janine. And Jeannie. Even Josh had been a good listener.

Through it all, Mark had been absent, really. To him, my problem hadn't seemed too important.

And he had become the last person I wanted to share it with. My own boyfriend!

Not a good sign.

"You're right, I guess," Mark said. "It feels different than it used to."

"We did have fun."

Mark smiled. "Yeah. You'll still pass me funny notes in homeroom, right? I mean, just as a friend?"

"Okay."

We hugged, but just briefly. Like friends.

"I guess that's it?" Mark said. He looked toward downtown. "Do you want to . . . ?"

I shook my head. "I have tons of home-work."

"Me too. I'll miss . . . you know."

"Me too."

That was it. We had broken up. No fights. No crying.

I was amazed.

Mark was backing away now, toward his house. "Hey, look at it this way: At least we'll still be King and Queen of the Seventh Grade!"

He turned, waving. I waved back.

"Right!" I said cheerfully.

The truth? I wasn't sure about that either.

CHAPTER 13

Tuesday

Today was the wrap-up of the first
annual Kids' Color War.

First? You sound like you want more than one.
Don't you, Mallory?

Sure, Stacey. When pigs fly.

"No, Suzi, you *roll* the hoop on the ground," Stacey explained, "pushing it along with the stick."

Suzi Barrett ignored her. Holding the guide stick in the air, she spun the plastic hoop around her waist and started shimmying. "Oh, I like to dance, I have ants in my pants!" she sang in a silly, high-pitched voice.

Her teammates were cracking up.

"Okay," Stacey said, crossing out the event on her Official BSC Kids' Color War Scorecard. "The hoop-rolling contest has now become a hoop dance!"

Not far away, against the baseball backstop, Mallory was helping Jake Kuhn onto a pair of stilts. "All I have to do is walk into the outfield?"

"It's harder than it looks," Mallory explained.

"Right," snickered her brother Adam, who was waiting his turn. "Maybe for Jake."

"What's that supposed to mean?" Jake snapped.

"Nothing," Adam replied.

Jake was on the stilts now, leaning against the chain-link fence. He trained his eyes forward. "Just you wait," he murmured.

Mallory gently pulled him upright, holding

onto the stilts. "On your mark . . . get set . . . *go!*"

She released her grip. Jake's right foot — along with the stilt — lunged forward and slightly to the right.

His left foot (and stilt) followed, slightly to the left.

"You're doing it!" Mallory shouted.

"Go, Jake!" screamed Marilyn Arnold, Jake's green-team partner.

Right.

Left.

With each step, Jake's legs spread farther apart. Finally he just stood still, wobbling, about to do a split.

Rrrrrrrip! went his pants. Right up the middle.

He tumbled to the ground.

Adam and Buddy Barrett, both on the red team, were doubled over, laughing.

Poor Jake. He was so embarrassed he started to cry.

"Okay, red team next!" Stacey shouted.

Guess what? Jake was soon laughing too. Neither Adam nor Buddy could travel any farther.

Nor could the black-team members, Patsy Kuhn and Shea Rodowsky.

Marilyn, however, made it all the way to center field.

"Green team, one point!" Stacey announced.

Across Brenner Field, a safe distance from everyone else, Kristy was holding a Nerf football toss. Four-year-old Jamie Newton was standing behind the throw line, which was a yardstick. He was winding his arm as if the Nerf ball were a baseball.

"Don't try to overpower it," Kristy warned.

"This is going to go so-o-o far," Jamie promised.

"Okay, Jamie, throw!" Kristy said.

Jamie kept winding. "I'm going to throw it across the whole field!"

"Jamieeee, hurry up!" urged Lindsey DeWitt, his teammate.

Jamie gritted his teeth and threw. The ball flipped into the air and landed behind him.

Lindsey quickly picked it up. "My turn."

"Good try, Jamie," Kristy said.

Jamie turned and walked to a tree. Silently he sat down. Then he burst into tears.

"Time-out!" Kristy ran to him. "Hey, pal, are you okay?"

"Kristyyyyyy, look!" Lindsey yelled.

Kristy peered over her shoulder. The football was bouncing way out in the field. "Sorry, Lindsey, I can't measure that. I called a time-out."

"I didn't hear it!" Lindsey protested.

"Well, go again," Kristy said.

"*I wanna go ho-o-o-ome!*" Jamie cried.

"Look, you can have another chance too," Kristy said.

"What about us?" bellowed Linny, who was waiting his turn. "You have to give *us* two chances too!"

"Fine," said Kristy.

"But I'll never throw it that far again," Lindsey complained.

"Crybaby," Linny taunted.

Lindsey picked up the Nerf ball and threw it at Linny. He caught it and threw it back. The ball bounced away and Jackie Rodowsky, Linny's teammate, picked it up. "War!" he cried.

"Give it back!" Kristy commanded.

Too late. The entire Color War soon degenerated into a free-for-all game of Nerf dodgeball. All the other activities stopped as kids jumped in.

Stacey was running around, yelling. So was Mallory.

Kristy had reached her limit.

And that is not a pretty sight.

"I HAVE HAD ENOUGH!" she shouted. "THIS ENTIRE COLOR WAR IS HEREBY — "

HO-O-O-O-ONK! H-O-O-O-ONK!

The loud horn made everyone turn toward the street.

The Stevensons' minivan was pulling up to

the curb. When it stopped, Abby jumped out and waved. "The prizes are here!"

Instant stampede. Every single Color War team ran to the minivan.

Mrs. Stevenson was walking around to the back of the van. "I hope you appreciate this," she said. "Do you have any idea how hard it is to *drive* here from New York City — even if you beat rush hour?"

She kept complaining (but in a friendly, teasing way) as she pulled open the door.

The back of the minivan was stuffed with big cardboard boxes — at least a dozen of them. On each of them was printed the logo of Mrs. Stevenson's publishing company.

"Wo-o-ow," said Suzi. "Are those for us?"

"Nope," Stacey replied. "They're for the charity chosen by the winning team."

"Well, maybe a few bonus books for the participants," Mrs. Stevenson said with a wink. "Right, girls?"

Kristy smiled. "Maybe."

"YEEEEEAAAAAAA!"

Stacey, Mallory, and Kristy had never seen kids so excited about books. The three teams raced back onto the field.

The final day of the Kids' Color War ended without a hitch.

The score? A tie. (At least, that was what Kristy claimed. Stacey says they crunched the numbers a bit, so no one would be disappointed.)

As a result, three different charities received brand-new children's books that week.

And so did our charges.

Kristy? She was already planning next year's Color War.

She never gives up.

CHAPTER 14

"You can throw it any way you want," Mark shouted to the orange-, white-, and blue-suited kids lined up on the basketball court. "Underhand, backward, jumping, standing on your head — as long as you're behind the foul line!"

This was ironic. On the second-to-last day of the SMS Color War, Mark was working harder than I was.

I felt funny sitting in the bleachers as a spectator. Most of my friends were busy in the gym or outside. Kristy was in a rope-climbing event and Jeannie was in a "Design a Color War Logo" contest (the winning entry to be used in next year's war). Stacey was trouncing everybody in a math contest. Josh was playing Speed Chess. But I had no events scheduled. I guess, in a way, that was a sign that the Color War was a success. The orange team was running on its own steam now.

So were the other teams. I think every kid in

every grade had participated in at least one event.

The score? White 45, Blue 50, and Orange 49.

Close. Very close. But I had confidence.

Mark caught my glance for a moment and waved. I smiled and waved back.

Another ironic thing. Now that we'd broken up, I liked Mark better. I didn't have to be angry about broken dates. I wasn't worried how he felt about me.

I was free to concentrate on all my other problems.

Like my future.

Now that it was Thursday, now that I'd had two whole days to think clearly, what had I decided?

Nothing.

Zero for two.

I still didn't know what to tell Mrs. Amer.

I still didn't know what to say to Josh.

I have to give Mrs. Amer credit. She wasn't pressuring me at all. Whenever I saw her in the hallway, she just smiled reassuringly.

Josh, on the other hand, was treating me as if I were the Queen of Cooties.

This was growing old. Very old. If Josh really liked me, why wasn't he saying anything? He must have known Mark was out of the picture. I hadn't had the nerve — or the time — to tell anyone, but it had to be obvious. Mark and I were no longer holding hands and hanging out together.

Was Josh playing hard to get? If so, it was working. Was he scared? Shy? Was he just waiting for the right time? Or had he given up, figuring I already hated him for waiting so long?

I was overthinking again.

I had to talk to him. Now.

I slid along the bleacher seats, closer to Josh's Speed Chess tournament.

I didn't have to wait long.

"Yyyyyyes! Checkmate!"

Josh leaped out of his seat, his fist thrust in the air. (How modest.)

"One point for Orange!" Mr. Kingbridge shouted through his megaphone.

"All right, Josh!" I shouted.

Josh took a bow in my direction.

I gestured toward the space next to me on the bleachers.

Josh looked left and right, then pointed to himself with an exaggerated gesture and mouthed, "Me?"

You bet. And now! I wanted to say.

Instead, I just nodded.

Josh bounded up the bleacher steps and sat next to me. "I slaughtered the guy," he announced. "And he's in eighth grade."

"Great," I said. "So, you're talking to me?"

"Talking?"

"Yeah. I mean, we've barely said a word to each other since we won our race. So . . . hi."

Josh gulped. "Right. Hi. Well, I guess it's been — I've been — with the — and the — you know . . ."

His voice trailed off. He gave me a sheepish look.

Together we blurted out, "So, how about those Mets?"

We both started laughing.

"You seem nervous, Josh," I said.

"Me, nevous? Nerver!" Josh shot back. "I mean . . ."

"You haven't come near me in days."

"Why should I come near you?" Josh winced. "I didn't mean that. I meant, I haven't had the need to — and Mark —"

"I thought you were mad at me. Or scared or something."

"Scared? Don't be ridiculous. I mean, mad is ridiculous too. Scared or mad." Josh's foot was tapping like crazy. "Well, maybe just mad. You know what I mean. *Why are you asking me so many questions?*"

"What questions? I haven't asked you any —"

"Yes! Okay? The answer is yes!"

"The answer to what?"

"I like you! All right? Are you happy? I think

about you all the time! I'd kiss the ground you walk on if it wouldn't ruin my orthodontia. Is that why you called me up here? To humiliate me?"

"Humiliate you? Is that the way you feel?" I asked.

"No!" Josh declared. "Actually, I feel great. I really do!"

"Well, so do I!"

Josh looked stunned. "You do?"

"Of course I do."

It was the truth. I felt as if I were flying.

"You mean, you . . . you don't think I'm, like, a total dork?"

"No. I've never thought that, Josh."

"Because, I don't know if you know this, and you're probably going to laugh at me, and it's okay if you do because I know it sounds stupid, but I've liked you from the moment I saw the back of your head."

I felt myself blushing. "What did you do when I turned around?"

"I got over it."

I pretended to be angry. I gave him a push.

But I felt absolutely electric inside.

"Joke!" Josh exclaimed. "Look, you don't have to take this seriously, okay? We can be the way we've always been. I'm not going to go psycho on you — you know, camp out on your lawn, make crank calls to Mark or anything —"

"Josh, what are you talking about?"

"I knew I should have kept my mouth shut," Josh barreled on. "Shira and Joanna and Jeannie were wrong. They said I should tell you everything, but I said no. Why make your life more complicated? I mean, you and Mark, Mark and you, fine. I can deal with it."

He didn't know.

"Josh. Slow down. Mark and I broke up."

Josh stared at me, dumbfounded, as if I'd just spoken in Greek. "What?"

"I thought you knew."

"Uh-uh." A smile crept across his face. "Was it because of *me*?"

"Well . . . not exactly."

"That's fine. 'Not exactly' is fine. I'll take it." Josh swallowed hard. He looked me squarely in the eye. "So, what does this mean?"

"I don't know, Josh. I guess that's kind of what I wanted to talk about."

"Can you and me . . . you and I . . . be, you know, more than just friend and friend?"

I shrugged. "I don't know. You can't just *declare* it. It sort of has to develop."

"Okay. Can we try?"

"I guess."

"I mean, it might make things a little complicated if you go back to eighth grade —"

Clunk.

"Ugh, did you have to remind me?"

"Sorry! I didn't mean to upset —" Josh cut himself off. "Wait. What did you mean, 'remind you'? Don't tell me. You are?"

"Are what?"

"Going back."

"No!"

"No, you're not?"

"No! I mean, no, I don't know!"

Suddenly all the Color War noise was crowding in on me. Screams and cheers and thuds and squeaks and bullhorn voices . . .

"Can we walk?" I asked.

"Sure."

Josh and I grabbed our jackets. Soon we were strolling in the school parking lot, within view of the outdoor Color War activities on the playing field.

"I'm supposed to know by now," I said. "Tomorrow's the big meeting with Mrs. Amer and my parents. What am I going to say? I can't make up my mind. What do *you* think I should do?"

"Me?"

"Sure. Everyone else has given me an opinion. I might as well hear yours."

Josh fell silent for a moment. We paced between the cars. I could see one of the teachers giving us a wary look, but I ignored it.

"Okay, two things," Josh finally said. "One. Do you think you can do it? Two. Will it make you happy to do it? If you can say yes to both, then go to eighth grade."

"That's not an opinion!"

"You don't need another one. This is your decision to make."

"You sound like Stacey."

"Well, Stacey's right."

I sighed. Josh was right too. No one had phrased it quite the way he had. No one had made the questions so clear.

"Okay, question one." I thought hard for awhile. "I guess I can catch up. If I work incredibly hard. With tutors. All the time."

Josh shrugged. "You're no dummy, Claudia. And your friends'll be there to help. They're smart too."

"Okay, then, number two. Will I be happy? How can I? I'll be losing you guys — you and Jeannie and Shira and Joanna."

"Look, when you were sent back a grade, your eighth-grade friends were there for you, weren't they?"

"Sure."

"Well, we're not going anywhere. If you move up, we'll be there for you too."

I almost choked up. I had to swallow a big lump.

Josh was looking at me calmly. Not a trace of nervousness. I believed what he said. I should have believed it all along. But somehow, hearing it from him and seeing his face made it all seem real.

Suddenly I felt as if a tremendous metal clamp had been loosened from my shoulders.

"So?" Josh said.

"Well, yes to one and yes to two, I guess."

Josh gave me a sad half smile. "Then I guess your decision is made."

I nodded slowly. "Yeah. I guess it is."

CHAPTER 15

"Yo, Claudia! Orange rules!"

"See you outside, Claudia?"

"*O-range! O-range! O-range!*"

"Go *blue!*"

"Boo Blue!"

"All *ri-i-i-i-ight*, White!"

"Orange you glad you're not Orange?"

The voices were echoing up and down the hallways. Heading toward the gym for the final Color War events. To me, they were like a tape. A tape playing in some distant room. I wasn't really there.

I was on my way to Mrs. Amer's office.

Mom and Dad were probably already there, waiting. So was Mr. Kingbridge. He had insisted on being involved with my decision.

I felt as if I were heading for some underground spy meeting to decide the fate of the world.

Which, in a funny way, was true.

True for *my* world.

I learned another word today, from Mary Anne. *Stoic.* People used to describe Mimi with that word, and I always thought it meant "old." But it doesn't. It means "not showing your true feelings."

Well, some of my friends had been pretty stoic when I'd told them about my decision. They hadn't tried to change my mind. They hadn't cried or yelled at me. In fact, everyone had hugged me and said I'd done the right thing. Even Mark.

After school they'd all gathered around my locker to wish me luck. I smiled stoically and marched to the guidance office.

Now, as I approached it, I was having second thoughts. And third and fourth thoughts.

I felt my body temperature drop as I neared Mrs. Amer's door. *Go for it, Kishi!* I told myself.

"Claudia, hello!" called Mrs. Amer. "Have a seat."

Four familiar pairs of eyes were staring at me. Mom's. Dad's. Mrs. Amer's. Mr. Kingbridge's. Everyone was present and ready.

I sat down. I forced a smile.

"Well, Claudia," Mrs. Amer began, "I know you have had quite a week, but . . . here we all are."

"Uck." I meant to say, "Uh-huh," but my mouth felt like cardboard.

"Would you like a glass of water?" Mr. Kingbridge asked me.

"I'm going to do it!" I blurted out. "Switch, I mean. To eighth grade."

My dad looked as if he were about to applaud. My mom was beaming. Mr. Kingbridge looked shocked.

But Mrs. Amer just nodded cautiously. "I know there are a lot of us here and only one of you. I don't want you to feel intimidated into doing this, Claudia. It's a big choice and it has to be completely yours."

"It is! You don't know how many ways I've been thinking about this. With my left brain. With my right brain. In my sleep. I'm ready. Totally. I'm going to do it, Mrs. Amer. And I'm going to do it well."

There.

I'd said it.

No turning back now.

Eighth grade or bust.

I thought I was going to fall off the chair.

"Whew," said Mr. Kingbridge.

Mrs. Amer was grinning. "I know you'll do it well, dear. Mr. Kingbridge and I have no doubt. Nor do your parents."

"None at all," my father said softly.

I don't know why, but that made me want to cry.

But I didn't. I was stoic.

"The marking period ends soon, so that'll be a natural time to switch," Mrs. Amer said. "But we can start the tutoring right away." She pushed a sheet of paper across the table toward my parents and me. On it was a tentative tutoring schedule. All my eighth-grade teachers-to-be had signed up to help me. "Will this be okay for you?"

The tutoring sessions were mostly after school and on Saturdays. I'd have to cut down on baby-sitting, but at least I wouldn't have to miss BSC meetings. My parents and I agreed to the schedule.

When we were finished, everyone rose and shook hands. I felt as if we'd just signed an international peace treaty.

"Congratulations, Your Majesty," Mr. Kingbridge said with a broad smile. "Now, shall we return to the festivities?"

"Yes, my loyal slave!" I replied.

My mom looked mortified. *"Claudia!"*

"Next week the royal treatment ends," I explained. "I have to live it up now."

Dad chuckled. Mr. Kingbridge gave a good-natured shrug.

We said our good-byes. I said mine very quickly.

I had to run out before I changed my mind.

On the way to the gym, I could feel myself becoming lighter. By the time I reached it I could barely feel my feet touching the ground.

Stacey was the first to see me. She ran to me. "Did you do it?"

"Yup."

"YEEEEEEEEEEAAAAAA!" She almost broke my eardrums.

We didn't have time to chat. I was scheduled for MUSIKWIZ, which involved listening to a song and guessing the name of the group.

I lost that one to this genius sixth-grader who plays in a garage band.

But I won the Snickers-eating competition (which was my idea, of course) and also a pin-the-guitar-on-Elvis contest, except that was called a tie even though Alan Gray was peeking under his blindfold and I protested the decision.

I was so-o-o-o mad. The score was close. Too close to be jeopardized by a cheater.

I paced in a corner of the gym. I was eyeing Alan, who was now rummaging through his gym bag by the door.

Josh found me in my corner. "What's up?" he asked.

"Alan cheated," I grumped. "If he costs us the win, I will kill him."

"Will Alan Gray please report to the sprint line?" Mr. Kingbridge called from outside.

"Don't worry about him," Josh said.

He swung his backpack around and pulled out a pair of grungy-looking track shoes.

On them were scribbled the words A. GRAY.

My jaw fell open. "You didn't!"

Josh nodded. "I saw what he did to you."

Alan was dumping the contents of his gym bag onto the ground. Candy wrappers and baseball cards flew everywhere.

Mr. Kingbridge's voice boomed: *"Alan, the sprint is about to —"*

"Coming!" Alan shouted.

He clomped outside to the starting line.

In his old, clunky work boots.

Josh looked at me. I looked at him.

"That was an awful, sneaky trick," I said.

Josh smiled. "I know."

We burst out laughing. Howling. We sank to the floor, leaning against each other.

When we calmed down, I leaned my head on Josh's shoulder and we gazed into the gym. We were sitting against a tile wall in a secluded area on the side of the bleachers.

"Well," I said, half sighing.

Josh nodded. "Well."

I sat up and smiled at him. "So . . . what do we do now?"

"We? You mean, like, we in terms of *us*?"

"Yeah."

"I don't know," Josh said with a shrug. "What do *you* want to do?"

"I don't know. What do *you* want to do?"

"This." Josh leaned closer to me, as if he'd

noticed something odd on my face.

But then he kept leaning. Until his face was so close I couldn't focus.

Then I felt his lips softly press mine.

I was shocked.

Stunned.

But I didn't want to move an inch.

Instead, I closed my eyes.

And I realized that all my decisions over the last twenty-four hours had been good ones.

All of them.

Josh pulled gently away. "You don't mind?"

"No."

"So does this mean we can have, like, a date? Maybe . . . tonight, after your meeting? We can get into a PG-13 movie. They never check me."

"Sure."

Josh was grinning. He wasn't the only one. So were Shira, Joanna, and Jeannie, directly across the gym from us. They were looking away, giggling. Trying to make it seem as if they hadn't noticed a thing.

Josh saw them too. We waved. They waved back and scooted away.

Josh and I stayed where we were until the contests were over. Soon all three classes were filing into the gym. Mr. Kingbridge, clutching a clipboard, walked to a lectern that had been set up under one of the baskets. The other teachers surrounded him.

"Attention, please," Mr. Kingbridge announced over the mike. "I have the final scores."

Squeals. Yelps. Shushes.

"White, sixty-five . . . Blue, seventy-one . . ."

A huge cheer went up from the eighth-graders. (Well, not all of them. Alan Gray was sitting by himself against the door, scowling.)

Mr. Kingbridge quieted everyone down, then continued, "And Orange . . . seventy-three!"

Josh and I practically leaped to the ceiling. We wrapped our arms around each other, screaming at the top of our lungs. The gym practically shook with cheering.

"Attention!" Mr. Kingbridge boomed. "Ms. Streeter is here from the Stoneybrook Chamber of Commerce. She has a check, which will be presented to the orange team's chosen organization, the Stoneybrook Adult Literacy Program. To accept this check on behalf of the seventh grade, I would like to invite to the lecturn someone who defined the spirit of this Color War, whose work for the orange team was absolutely tireless . . . your Queen of the Seventh Grade, Claudia Kishi!"

"Yyyyyeaa!" Josh shouted. "CLAU-DI-*AHHH*! CLAU-DI-*AHHH*! CLAU-DI-*AHHH*!"

Instantly everyone was chanting. It was so

embarrassing. I must have looked like the inside of a watermelon.

Oh, well, at least red goes with orange.

I took the check from Ms. Streeter, thanked her, and waved it above my head to the crowd.

I realized this was my last act as Queen.

My stomach sank.

Someone started playing a rock CD over the loudspeakers. A tune by Blade, one of my favorite groups.

Now everyone was chanting my name to the beat of the song.

I could see my BSC friends in the center of the bleachers, jumping and cheering. Kristy was pumping her fist in the air. Mary Anne was blubbering away.

Shira, Joanna, and Jeannie were busy organizing a kick line in the bleachers with a bunch of seventh-graders.

Mark, in the top row with his buddies, was grinning at me proudly.

Josh was not where we'd been sitting anymore. I spotted him by the door to the hallway. Smiling. Dancing.

I laughed out loud.

Okay, so I'd miss being Queen. I'd miss the attention.

But I could deal with it.

I tucked the check into my pocket. And I began to dance too.

Dear Reader,

I've received lots of letters from readers who are having friendship problems, especially problems involving having two very different groups of friends. Kids want to know how they can stay friends with classmates who are different from each other or who do not know each other well. Claudia thinks she's going to face this very problem in *Claudia Makes Up Her Mind*, but she finds that she doesn't have to choose one group of friends over the other. By making friends in the seventh grade, she has simply widened her circle of friends.

Many people have different kinds of friends — friends from school, family friends, friends from a sports team — and it's not necessary for all of your friends to be friends with each other. What's important is that *you* enjoy spending time with them. When I was in eighth grade, I had my neighborhood friends (including my best friend Beth) with whom I would hang out after school and during the summer. I also had my school friends, kids I mostly saw in my classes or in the afternoons during after-school activities, such as art club. Some of my friends didn't even know each other, but they were *my* friends and they were all important to me in different ways.

Happy reading,

Ann M Martin

L. GODWIN

Ann M. Martin

About the Author

ANN MATTHEWS MARTIN was born on August 12, 1955. She grew up in Princeton, NJ, with her parents and her younger sister, Jane.

Although Ann used to be a teacher and then an editor of children's books, she's now a full-time writer. She gets the ideas for her books from many different places. Some are based on personal experiences. Others are based on childhood memories and feelings. Many are written about contemporary problems or events.

All of Ann's characters, even the members of the Baby-sitters Club, are made up. (So is Stoneybrook.) But many of her characters are based on real people. Sometimes Ann names her characters after people she knows, other times she chooses names she likes.

In addition to the Baby-sitters Club books, Ann Martin has written many other books for children. Her favorite is *Ten Kids, No Pets* because she loves big families and she loves animals. Her favorite Baby-sitters Club book is *Kristy's Big Day*. (By the way, Kristy is her favorite baby-sitter!)

Ann M. Martin now lives in New York with her cats, Gussie and Woody. Her hobbies are reading, sewing, and needlework — especially making clothes for children.

Notebook Pages

This Baby-sitters Club book belongs to _____.

I am _____ years old and in the _____

grade.

The name of my school is _____.

I got this BSC book from _____.

I started reading it on _____ and

finished reading it on _____.

The place where I read most of this book is _____.

My favorite part was when _____.

If I could change anything in the story, it might be the part when

_____.

My favorite character in the Baby-sitters Club is _____.

The BSC member I am most like is _____

because _____.

If I could write a Baby-sitters Club book it would be about ____

_____.

#113 Claudia Makes Up Her Mind

In *Claudia Makes Up Her Mind*, Claudia faces many big decisions. For instance, she has to choose between staying in seventh grade or moving back to eighth grade. I wanted Claudia to choose _____ because _____ _____. If I had a chance to switch into a grade older than mine, I would choose to _____ _____. Claudia also has to choose between her boyfriend Mark and her friend Josh, who has a big crush on her. If I were Claudia, I would have chosen to go out with _____ because _____ _____. Claudia realizes Josh is the right guy for her. The right person for me is _____. I like this person because _____ _____.

CLAUDIA'S

A spooky sitting adventure.

Finger painting at 3...

Sitting for two of my favorite charges --
Jamie and Lucy Newton.

SCRAPBOOK

...oil painting
at 13!

my family. Mom and Dad, me and
Janine... and we'll never forget Mimi.

Interior art by Angelo Tillery

Read all the books
about **Claudia**
in the Baby-sitters Club series
by Ann M. Martin

Look for #114

THE SECRET LIFE OF MARY ANNE SPIER

Sitting cross-legged on Dawn's bed, I dumped out the receipts. With the pen I'd been using to write out gift tags, I transferred prices from the receipts onto the empty bag. My heartbeat quickened as I kept adding. The list seemed almost endless. As I reached the bottom of the bag I had to write smaller and smaller to fit it all on.

The first time I added the numbers, I scratched out my answer. It had to be wrong. I could not possibly have spent that much money! Could I have? No! I added again and discovered that — as I thought — I had been mistaken. I'd actually spent five dollars *more* than the first number I'd reached.

The next two times I added I came up with the same astronomical figure — three times the amount of money I had saved.

Three times!

I didn't understand how this could have happened. At the mall, it just hadn't seemed as if I was spending that much. Maybe it was the credit card. When you don't actually see the money leaving your hand it doesn't seem as though you're really spending money.

What should I do? What *could* I do? The gifts were already wrapped and under the tree. I couldn't take them back. I supposed it was possible, but I'd feel like such an idiot. What would I tell Sharon and Dad? "Never mind. These gifts were just a joke!" They'd think I was crazy. Dawn and Jeff would be here by Monday. They'd see all the gifts too.

Calm down, I urged myself. *So what if you have to pay a little interest?* How bad could it be?

It would probably be a good idea to find out.

THE BABY-SITTERS CLUB®

Collect them all!

More titles... ➤

❑ MG22873-0	#89	**Kristy and the Dirty Diapers**	$3.50
❑ MG22874-9	#90	**Welcome to the BSC, Abby**	$3.99
❑ MG22875-1	#91	**Claudia and the First Thanksgiving**	$3.50
❑ MG22876-5	#92	**Mallory's Christmas Wish**	$3.50
❑ MG22877-3	#93	**Mary Anne and the Memory Garden**	$3.99
❑ MG22878-1	#94	**Stacey McGill, Super Sitter**	$3.99
❑ MG22879-X	#95	**Kristy + Bart = ?**	$3.99
❑ MG22880-3	#96	**Abby's Lucky Thirteen**	$3.99
❑ MG22881-1	#97	**Claudia and the World's Cutest Baby**	$3.99
❑ MG22882-X	#98	**Dawn and Too Many Sitters**	$3.99
❑ MG69205-4	#99	**Stacey's Broken Heart**	$3.99
❑ MG69206-2	#100	**Kristy's Worst Idea**	$3.99
❑ MG69207-0	#101	**Claudia Kishi, Middle School Dropout**	$3.99
❑ MG69208-9	#102	**Mary Anne and the Little Princess**	$3.99
❑ MG69209-7	#103	**Happy Holidays, Jessi**	$3.99
❑ MG69210-0	#104	**Abby's Twin**	$3.99
❑ MG69211-9	#105	**Stacey the Math Whiz**	$3.99
❑ MG69212-7	#106	**Claudia, Queen of the Seventh Grade**	$3.99
❑ MG69213-5	#107	**Mind Your Own Business, Kristy!**	$3.99
❑ MG69214-3	#108	**Don't Give Up, Mallory**	$3.99
❑ MG69215-1	#109	**Mary Anne to the Rescue**	$3.99
❑ MG05988-2	#110	**Abby the Bad Sport**	$3.99
❑ MG05989-0	#111	**Stacey's Secret Friend**	$3.99
❑ MG05990-4	#112	**Kristy and the Sister War**	$3.99
❑ MG45575-3		**Logan's Story Special Edition Readers' Request**	$3.25
❑ MG47118-X		**Logan Bruno, Boy Baby-sitter**	
		Special Edition Readers' Request	$3.50
❑ MG47756-0		**Shannon's Story Special Edition**	$3.50
❑ MG47686-6		**The Baby-sitters Club Guide to Baby-sitting**	$3.25
❑ MG47314-X		**The Baby-sitters Club Trivia and Puzzle Fun Book**	$2.50
❑ MG48400-1		**BSC Portrait Collection: Claudia's Book**	$3.50
❑ MG22864-1		**BSC Portrait Collection: Dawn's Book**	$3.50
❑ MG69181-3		**BSC Portrait Collection: Kristy's Book**	$3.99
❑ MG22865-X		**BSC Portrait Collection: Mary Anne's Book**	$3.99
❑ MG48399-4		**BSC Portrait Collection: Stacey's Book**	$3.50
❑ MG69182-1		**BSC Portrait Collection: Abby's Book**	$3.99
❑ MG92713-2		**The Complete Guide to The Baby-sitters Club**	$4.95
❑ MG47151-1		**The Baby-sitters Club Chain Letter**	$14.95
❑ MG48295-5		**The Baby-sitters Club Secret Santa**	$14.95
❑ MG45074-3		**The Baby-sitters Club Notebook**	$2.50
❑ MG44783-1		**The Baby-sitters Club Postcard Book**	$4.95

Available wherever you buy books...or use this order form.

Scholastic Inc., P.O. Box 7502, Jefferson City, MO 65102

Please send me the books I have checked above. I am enclosing $_____
(please add $2.00 to cover shipping and handling). Send check or money order–
no cash or C.O.D.s please.

Name_____ Birthdate_____

Address_____

City_____State/Zip_____

BSC5962

THE BABY-SITTERS CLUB®

by Ann M. Martin

Collect and read these exciting BSC Super Specials, Mysteries, and Super Mysteries along with your favorite Baby-sitters Club books!

BSC Super Specials

❏ BBK44240-6	Baby-sitters on Board! Super Special #1	$3.95
❏ BBK44239-2	Baby-sitters' Summer Vacation Super Special #2	$3.95
❏ BBK43973-1	Baby-sitters' Winter Vacation Super Special #3	$3.95
❏ BBK42493-9	Baby-sitters' Island Adventure Super Special #4	$3.95
❏ BBK43575-2	California Girls! Super Special #5	$3.95
❏ BBK43576-0	New York, New York! Super Special #6	$4.50
❏ BBK44963-X	Snowbound! Super Special #7	$3.95
❏ BBK44962-X	Baby-sitters at Shadow Lake Super Special #8	$3.95
❏ BBK45661-X	Starring The Baby-sitters Club! Super Special #9	$3.95
❏ BBK45674-1	Sea City, Here We Come! Super Special #10	$3.95
❏ BBK47015-9	The Baby-sitters Remember Super Special #11	$3.95
❏ BBK48308-0	Here Come the Bridesmaids! Super Special #12	$3.95
❏ BBK22883-8	Aloha, Baby-sitters! Super Special #13	$4.50
❏ BBK69216-X	BSC in the USA Super Special #14	$4.50

BSC Mysteries

❏ BAI44084-5	#1 Stacey and the Missing Ring	$3.50
❏ BAI44085-3	#2 Beware Dawn!	$3.50
❏ BAI44799-8	#3 Mallory and the Ghost Cat	$3.50
❏ BAI44800-5	#4 Kristy and the Missing Child	$3.50
❏ BAI44801-3	#5 Mary Anne and the Secret in the Attic	$3.50
❏ BAI44961-3	#6 The Mystery at Claudia's House	$3.50
❏ BAI44960-5	#7 Dawn and the Disappearing Dogs	$3.50
❏ BAI44959-1	#8 Jessi and the Jewel Thieves	$3.50
❏ BAI44958-3	#9 Kristy and the Haunted Mansion	$3.50
❏ BAI45696-2	#10 Stacey and the Mystery Money	$3.50
❏ BAI47049-3	#11 Claudia and the Mystery at the Museum	$3.50

More titles ➡

The Baby-sitters Club books continued...

Available wherever you buy books...or use this order form.

Scholastic Inc., P.O. Box 7502, Jefferson City, MO 65102-7502

Please send me the books I have checked above. I am enclosing $ _____
(please add $2.00 to cover shipping and handling). Send check or money order
— no cash or C.O.D.s please.

Name_____Birthdate_____

Address _____

City_____State/Zip_____

Please allow four to six weeks for delivery. Offer good in the U.S. only. Sorry, mail orders are not
available to residents of Canada. Prices subject to change.